Mastering
the Art of
Witchcraft
Building a Practical Foundation

ABOUT THE AUTHOR

FRATER BARRABBAS TIRESIUS is a practicing ritual magician who has studied magic and the occult for over forty years. He believes that ritual magic is a discipline whose mystery is unlocked by continual practice and by occult experiences and revelations. Frater Barrabbas believes that traditional approaches should be balanced with creativity and experimentation, and that no occult or magical tradition is exempt from changes and revisions.

Over the years, he found that his practical magical discipline was the real source for all his creative efforts. That creative process helped him build and craft a unique and different kind of magical system, one that is quite unlike any other yet based on common Wiccan practices. So, despite its uniqueness this magical system is capable of being easily adapted and used by others.

Frater Barrabbas is also the founder of a magical order called the Order of the Gnostic Star and he is an elder and lineage holder in the Alexandrian tradition of Witchcraft.

Mastering the Art of Witchcraft
Building a Practical Foundation

Frater Barrabbas

Mastering the Art of Witchcraft: Building a Practical Foundation copyright © 2023 by Frater Barrabbas. All rights reserved. No part of this book may be reproduced in any manner whatsoever without written permission from Crossed Crow Books, except in the case of brief quotations embodied in critical articles and reviews.

First Printing. 2024.

Paperback ISBN: 978-1-959883-31-9
Hardcover ISBN: 978-1-959883-79-1
Library of Congress Control Number on file.

Cover design by Wycke Malliway.
Edited by Jason Winslade.
Typesetting by Gianna Rini.

Disclaimer: Crossed Crow Books, LLC does not participate in, endorse, or have any authority or responsibility concerning private business transactions between our authors and the public. Any internet references contained in this work were found to be valid during the time of publication, however, the publisher cannot guarantee that a specific reference will continue to be maintained. This book's material is not intended to diagnose, treat, cure, or prevent any disease, disorder, ailment, or any physical or psychological condition. The author, publisher, and its associates shall not be held liable for the reader's choices when approaching this book's material. The views and opinions expressed within this book are those of the author alone and do not necessarily reflect the views and opinions of the publisher.

Published by:
Crossed Crow Books, LLC
6934 N Glenwood Ave, Suite C
Chicago, IL 60626
www.crossedcrowbooks.com

Printed in the United States of America.

Dedication

This book is dedicated to all the beginners who seek to build for themselves an independent practice of Witchcraft, and to Rebecca, who first inspired me to write this book, and to Thraicie, owner of Eye of Horus bookstore who told me to write it, to the Malliway brothers who made this work possible, to my wife Joni, who taught me how to write books, and to Lynxa, my feline muse.

Acknowledgments

Many thanks to Keith Ward for his artistic assistance and visions, to the staff at Crossed Crow Books, and to my secret muse, who dropped the table of contents for this book into my lap.

I would like to also acknowledge Paul Huson, whose book *Mastering Witchcraft: A Practical Guide for Witches, Warlocks and Covens* so inspired me back when I was starting out. May this work be an inspiration for today's beginners as Paul's book was for me.

CONTENTS

Note by the Author . . . . *xi*

CHAPTER 1: FIRST STEPS TOWARD INDEPENDENT WITCHCRAFT 1

Tradition vs. Independence. 2
Polytheism, Pantheon, and Culture. 6
Location: A Very Private Practice. 11
Acquiring the Accouterments of the Craft 16
Preparations for the Work 20

CHAPTER 2: FOUNDATIONAL PRACTICES AND TOOLS 23

Meditation and Trance. 24
Four Elemental Tools and Their Use. 30
Magic Circle, Altar, and Shrine 32
Circle Consecration Rite: Making Sacred Space. 35
Ritual for Circle Consecration 37
Building a Lunar and Solar Calendar 40
Developing Hymns and Invocations to the Deities. 45
Divination Techniques 46

CHAPTER 3: LITURGICAL PRACTICES PERFORMED IN SACRED SPACE 49

Votive Offerings, Prayers, Meditation, Seasonal Practices . .52
Full Moon Esbats. 54
Seasonal Sabbats 57
Invocation of Deities and Communion Rites 60
Developing a Shrine of Deities and Ancestors 63
Self-Dedication Rite 66
Dedication Rite 67

Chapter 4: Practical Magical Workings Part One 69

Timing, Ethics, and Magical Considerations 73
Tool Consecration Rite. 76
Magic Pentagram—Basic Energy Working. 78
Sigil Magic: Signs, Seals, and Witch Marks 84
Basic Ritual Spell Structures. 86
Divination Session 90

Chapter 5: Practical Magical Workings Part Two 94

Binding and Releasing: Symbolic Cord Magic 97
Art of Incantation: Words of Power 104
Poppet Creation and Magical Uses. 107
Gathering and Dispensing Magical Energy 111
Seeking the Aid of Deities and Spirits 113
Grand Invocation of Powers. 115

Chapter 6: Developing an Advanced Magical Practice 120

Divination 122
Witchcraft History and Folklore 123
Mythology/Theology 124
Qabalah/Kabbalah 124
Duration and Qualifications for Foundational Work. . . . 126
Approaching the *For Witches* Series Study. 129
Competency vs. Expertise. 132
Witchcraft Path: Living Religion and Magic 134

Appendix: Pantheon Development. 137
Bibliography. 147
Index 149

NOTE BY THE AUTHOR

I NEVER WANTED TO WRITE A BOOK on Witchcraft for beginners. I had basically thought that this literary niche was well-stocked with all kinds of books taken from every angle that one could possibly entertain. There are also a lot of online media consisting of books, rituals, articles, videos, and websites that specialize in online training. The whole market of Witchcraft media appears to be oriented toward introducing and training, not to mention selling various tools, products, and crafts to the would-be beginning Witch. If I wrote a book for beginners, I would only be one of many thousands cluttering up a burgeoning marketplace, both online and in printed books.

My place, I had thought, in the task of writing books, was to supply the more experienced Witch who already knew the basics with a more advanced approach to the art of Witchcraft. That is why I have published five books in the *For Witches* series to cover all the topics and areas of practice that are not to be found in either beginner books or the basic traditional practices found in covens throughout the U.S. These were five areas that are not typically found in books and materials written about Witchcraft, so I had a good market niche to write and publish my books. However, in publishing books that are not for beginners, I left out a large population of people who are seeking to become a Witch, and who would find my book series useful and even inspiring.

When I attended the convention Paganicon in March of 2023 in Paganistan, I discovered that not only were my books and writings significant and popular to the Witchcraft community, but that several individuals had asked me if there were any books or materials that I could provide for the beginner. Of course, I demurred at first, but after several requests for this kind of book, and the owner of a local bookstore asked if I could write something like this, I then relented. I began to seriously consider writing such a book. I know, it was astonishing to even think about this, and it goes against my basic premise as an author; but after careful consideration, I believe that I saw the need and the solution.

While there are a lot of books for beginners in the market, these books are not written for that special person who wants to practice their Craft outside or in lieu of a coven. Certainly, there are books for the solitary Witch, and in fact, there are more of them out there than books written for covens or groups. Yet, as I perused the market for books, I found that many of them were incomplete and did not prepare a person for a solitary practice that focused on both a religious and a magical path as a single discipline. Many of these books focused on one topical area at the expense of other areas. Either they presented Witchcraft as a religious form of Wicca, focusing on the basic religious practices, or they presented Witchcraft as magical technology, with an emphasis on energy work, folk magic, divination, tool workings, or other popular themes. Some were even based on *Harry Potter*. I didn't find a single book that presented a whole and complete Witchcraft discipline that would provide the proper foundation for accessing my more advanced works.

Even in the various traditions of Witchcraft, which are starting to become a bit more popular than previously, the basic regimen of training seldom includes what I would consider the basic set of magical skills and capabilities. Additionally, the members of a traditional coven are engaged in group workings, and individual magical workings and worship are not really encouraged. I know this because when I meet young Witches who are part of a traditional coven, their knowledge of what I consider to be the basic occult and magical teachings is either superficial or missing altogether. What I was taught and

Note by the Author

developed in my days as a beginner seems to be omitted in the training and work for the beginner in the present age.

These discoveries have led me to reconsider writing a book for beginners. What I want to do is to present a discipline that a beginner can adopt as they build their own personal system of Witchcraft worship and magic. Like my other books on Witchcraft, the structure and table of contents for this book materialized to me once I decided to write this kind of book, which was my literary muse's way of inspiring and pushing me to write it. The rest is written here for your examination and use.

Frater Barrabbas

CHAPTER 1

FIRST STEPS TOWARD INDEPENDENT WITCHCRAFT

It is often said that every beginner must start somewhere with something to make any measurable progress. The task at the beginning of a study of Witchcraft must include three basic strategies. Individuals must study various sources of information via books, internet media, and other types of information to get an adequate background. This is because Witches are not people of the book; they are more like people of the library.

Students will need to collect the tools and materials and make a space available for this work, whether temporary or permanent, so they can practice the rituals and ceremonies associated with the Craft. The final task is to regularly and frequently practice the rituals, spells, and ceremonies. Students will need to experiment with these rites and practices so that a body of rituals, ceremonies, and workings will be produced. That body of lore will be developed over time, continually revised, refined, and hopefully, become a living and breathing personal tradition. This will become their personal Book of Shadows—ever-growing and never completed.

In addition to developing an informational background, building lore, collecting tools, and creating a space to perform this work, a beginner should also consider taking a more independent approach to their Craft and developing a cultural context for that practice. A discipline that is managed daily, weekly, monthly, and seasonally is very important to adopt, and it will be the mechanism that will make Witchcraft become not only fully realized, but also a living tradition where religion and magic, spirit and body, life and death, light and darkness become an integral part of the seeker's life as a Witch.

The very final thing that a student should contemplate is a rite of dedication, made to a Deity or Deities that make up their chosen pantheon. Such a rite is both simple and profoundly significant, especially for someone who is not in a coven nor working toward achieving initiation grades. Even if a student already belongs to a coven, making a personal and independent dedication to specific Goddesses and Gods represents that there is a personal relationship with Deity that will become the main driver for all that occurs in the life of the student Witch. This is because we who are in the Craft, do our work, both religious and magical, with an alignment to a specific Deity.

We who are Witches seek to develop that connection with Deity and ultimately, we become so familiar with it that we will assume some of its characteristics into our own personality and beingness. That adjunct godhead in our mind and soul will be the real teacher, counselor, and spiritual intermediary for all those on the path, making our membership in a coven or community of secondary and lesser importance. This, then, is the real start to our Witchcraft avocation.

Tradition vs. Independence

Modern Witchcraft is essentially a social phenomenon where liturgical and magical workings are performed by a group. Whether that group is an established coven based on traditional practices or a loosely structured group that meets to perform the art of Witchcraft, what occurs is a group performance of rites or workings. This is also true regarding the seasonal celebrations, which often are performed by the community at large.

First Steps Toward Independent Witchcraft

Many books that are in print today which teach beginners how to practice Witchcraft are written with the assumption that there will be a group to perform these rites. Not all books are written for groups, however, and some are written for the solitary practitioner as well.

They all have one thing in common, and that is they do not present the practice of Witchcraft as a complete system and a seamless discipline that combines religious rites with magical workings. Most of the materials I have examined that introduce someone to the practice of Witchcraft are missing important and critical topics. Either they focus on one area, such as religious ceremonies, and discuss very little regarding the other topics, or they focus on divination, or some aspect of magic, and omit the religious perspectives. These omissions would make acquiring more advanced Witchcraft practices difficult or even impossible without the inclusion of everything that would be required for a well-rounded practice.

This is a malady that plagues traditional covens, loosely affiliated groups, and solitary practitioners. Neither books nor traditional coven practices seem to be able to pull together the practical lore for both liturgical rites and ceremonies and magical workings. When I was getting my training in Witchcraft practices, I received a body of lore, training, and a bibliography that would represent a comprehensive background in the art of Witchcraft. I know other folks back in the 1970s and 1980s who received such training, but today, it seems to be something of a missing step in the growing of a tradition. My hope is to remedy this by at least presenting what would be a solid regimen for the Witch in training so that such a person could tackle any other system of magic or occultism.

What is required of the beginning Witch, in my opinion, and whatever their status, is to develop an independent perspective, an inquiring mind, and a desire to perform experimental magical workings alone and in their own temple space. Such a perspective can be somewhat contrary to what passes for normal activity in a traditional coven or loosely affiliated group.

It seems almost antisocial to work alone and to experiment and discover new lore without input (or interference) from others. I believe that a group and its work have an important place, but also that a Witch must learn to perform their liturgies and magical workings separately from what the group that they belong to might seek to do. Self-reliance is a critical faculty for the beginning Witch to develop since an over-reliance on the group and its activities will likely minimize the level of growth and the development of new directions and lore.

Additionally, I cannot stress enough the importance that a Witch must possess their own magic and faith. Without learning to practice religion and magic in their own particular and individual way, that religion and magic will never really belong to them. Making a practice into a possession is what makes it both real and deeply internalized. Without that kind of effort, the practice will belong to the group and the tradition, but not to the individual. Only when Witches possess their own regimen and practice, through their individual and active use, will that discipline become truly their own. When Witches end their allegiance to a group or coven, and that event typically happens to nearly everyone, then they will pass into their world of solitary practice with hardly a ripple of regret or despair.

When I was a beginner—and at some point, we were all beginners—I had my own separate system of magic that I had been working on prior to joining a coven. I continued that work despite getting some pressure from my coven and its leaders that such work was considered extraneous and invalid if it did not receive proper authorization from the group, especially from its more experienced members. I did some demonstrations and that seemed to quiet my coven leaders, so I was able to continue my work without interference.

Later, when I had to leave that group because it had become untenable for me to remain a member, I had my own system of magic and worship to fall back on when working with a group was no longer available. Learning to be independent helped me to continue with my Witchcraft practices and avoid any lapses of support or help since I no longer needed that kind of assistance. Other Witches in my group did not fare as well as I did when they were either exiled or quit, and that is because I was prepared to operate as either a group leader or as a solitary practitioner. In the years after my expulsion from that coven, I have functioned in both roles, but I was able to continue my work until it achieved a level of maturity that made it useful to others.

If I could state anything that I had learned over the decades as the one most important thing that I had learned while practicing my Craft, I would have to say learning to be independent, open-minded, and willing to experiment on my own was the most important lesson. It is this very lesson that I impart to you so that you might learn to develop your practice in an independent manner and if necessary, completely outside of your defined tradition. This is because I have found that traditions are often artificial boundaries erected by the opinions and unverified constraints imposed by others who have never strayed from what they believe to be orthodoxy. In Witchcraft, there really is no orthodoxy. Everything associated with the Witchcraft tradition is in a stage of development and has been since its origins in the 1950s. Our faith is too young and underdeveloped to be constrained by any notions of orthodoxy.

One other item that I need to state in association with following an independent path is to always have some kind of peer group or close associates that you can discuss and get important feedback about your plans, ritual workings, and their results, and what you have learned from your workings. When I urge beginners to learn to be independent, I am not advocating that they isolate themselves from everyone. We all need a peer group to assess and judge what we are doing so we can keep from adopting erroneous and egotistic ideas about ourselves and our magic. Ego inflation is always a problem, especially for the solitary practitioner, so having some friends who can give you a sanity check regarding your opinions, beliefs, and work is an important possession. I would recommend that you continue to cultivate friends and associates as you develop your Craft.

So, you have the incentive to develop an independent approach to your Craft regarding worship and magical workings, and you have some friends with whom you can talk about these topics. The only other thing that you need is to determine the scope of your independent approach and to have a plan to move forward. We need to discuss these two topics regarding both the independent worship of the Witchcraft Deities and the kind and type of magical experiments that you will perform. We need to define the scope of the work and the stages or plan for development. The goal is to develop a Witchcraft practice that is thorough and complete, preparing you for greater development and aspirations. The scope is to determine the religious and cultural boundaries through which you desire to work.

Polytheism, Pantheon, and Culture

It is an unspoken rule that modern Witchcraft and Paganism cannot exist without some kind of corresponding culture. That means our Deities and practices should have some kind of cultural background or context with which to exist. Since Witchcraft is not a universal religion that can be transported anywhere and be readily used by anyone, it must therefore exist within a culture and a locality or place. This makes Witchcraft and Paganism, especially in the U.S., a traditional practice that is dependent on Deities associated with far-flung cultures, localities, and even languages not native to this geographic location. We don't have the luxury of living in a place where an antique non-Christian faith resides along with a supporting culture, language, and a locally invested mythology. We don't live in Wales, the highlands of Scotland, Latvia or northeastern Finland, and other pockets of Europe where some form of Pagan religious practice has survived or been revived from living remnants.

First Steps Toward Independent Witchcraft

Some of the earliest forms of Witchcraft used Celtic, Gaelic, Brythonic, or Welsh Deities and a bit or smattering of the language and antique folklore and bardic stories as their culture. Slightly later, some sought to revive Saxon Paganism, their Deities, calendric rite names, and bits of language to build a tradition. Most of these efforts, particularly those imported from the UK, were reconstructions that used a combination of the scant lore available and filled in the rest with creative imagination. What was produced was not particularly authentic or even legitimate, but like all constructs, it gained a life of its own.

Gardner aimed for the period of the High Middle Ages to produce an English version of Witchcraft, even though there were small, isolated pockets of similar practices located in fringe locations, like the Scottish Highlands, where some form of antique Pagan beliefs and magic still had an existence. Gardner didn't make use of these remnants because he didn't know about them. They were very obscure, secretive, and rare. The archaic and antique practices were likely found side-by-side with established Christian churches and practices, and often there was a mixture of old and new customs. It is likely that even many of these antique Pagan practices were revitalizations of a practice that had ceased to exist and only the remnants, such as some beliefs about non-Christian entities, folk magical practices, herbal and healing lore, and other surviving folklore persisted. What we would call indigenous European religions would hardly be recognized by modern Witches and Pagans in the U.S., but these holdovers from a previous age have an advantage over us modern urban or suburban practitioners.

What we lack is a religious and magical practice that has a fully functioning culture, language, traditional location, active myths, practices, ceremonies, and a body of people united in their faith. That advantage must be developed in some manner for us to function as polytheists engaging in a nature-based religion and magical practice. If we are divorced from the earth, then our so-called nature religion has as its foundation an extreme hypocrisy.

This means that we need to have a rural setting where we can commune with nature on a periodic basis, and we need to be able to approach such a natural setting with veneration, sensitivity, and openness to the ever-changing cycle of seasons, lunar phases, and the capriciousness of climate and weather. All the other attributes of a culture can be built or derived in some fashion, including a community, communal practices, and a shared language.

As modern Pagans and Witches, we live in a changing diaspora far from the homeland of our ancestors, but we carry their legacy in our hearts and souls, and we can use our creativity to build and develop what was lost. Still, the earth is where we must ground our faith and regenerate our nature-based sensibilities. Into it, we are born, and in it, we are interred at the end of life. This is true whether we live in a populous metropolitan area, the crowded suburbs, or the ever-expanding megapolises that are cluttering up our world. Where there is nature untrammeled, we are drawn to it, even for short durations. That is the way of the urban or suburban Witch.

Choosing a culture to vest one's practice in is to base it on what is in one's heart and soul. That might be a difficult thing to define, at least initially. Yet, for those who have not found a refuge in a popular mainstream creed, such as Christianity, Judaism, or Islam, or one of the many sectarian offshoots, they will sense a gravitation to one or many of the polytheistic Deities from the past, and with that affinity, they will also elect the associated culture.

Now that culture associated with the chosen Deities will likely be long past any kind of resurrection or reenactment, and what will be known will likely be scant or even nonexistent, unless it is one of the classical Deities, and then there will be a mythology, idolatrous images and artwork, characterizations, and associated accessories and symbols that will accompany it. There will also be a language that can be learned or approximated. Whatever information is available will be used to help build up a personalized cult of that Deity and its family, since a polytheistic Deity is never alone.

For instance, a lot of information is available about Apollo, Artemis, Zeus, Athena, Aphrodite, or Hera. Less is known about the Roman Deities, but they are compared to the Greek Deities and a kind of correspondence was determined. However, much less is known about Cernunnos or Herne, or the various Brythonic, Welsh, Gaelic, or Celtic Deities. Still, what is lacking in myths, stories, characterizations, and imagery can be replaced with the artifice of imagination. Whatever strikes a student's fancy regarding Deities will draw them to the culture and language. What is developed, however, doesn't need to be historically accurate or perfect regarding the chosen language, and in fact, only certain words that appeal to the ear and aesthetics of the student Witch need to be included in this work.

What is produced is an image of the chosen Deity or Deities, their mythic representations, stories (if any), preferred libations and food, prayers, hymns, and meditations. Additionally, some words or prayers in the language of the Deity's culture will function as words of power for these rites. When approaching this Deity, the Witch will give votive offerings, prayers, hymns, and invocations, and engage in a form of communion as a proper way of liturgically serving this Deity and functioning as its priest and congregation. As one gains insights, dreams, visions, and even paranormal observations from this kind of spiritual work, then the quality and depth of that lore will grow, be revised, and refined over time to become a fully realized religious practice. This process starts out simple and rudimentary, but it ends up being elegant and pleasing, but it is a personal cult of the Witch and is attended by them and their Deities alone.

Something very important to remember is that our own culture is rich with myths, old and modern, occult, and metaphysical beliefs, lists of angels, demons, mythical beasts, and various unusual practices that have many sources, and these are available to us. It is part of our heritage, even as a post-modern technology-based society where we also have a mountain of older and archaic beliefs and practices already embedded in our cultural world, and these can and should be extracted and renewed to be part of our Witchcraft practice. You don't have to be a Christian to consort with angels or borrow religious ideas or practices and import them into your construct of Witchcraft practices. All these systems of belief are available to be used to build up your own practices, both magical and religious. When it comes to developing your own personal religious cult, whatever works and seems aesthetically pleasing to you is available for your use. In the domain of ideas about spiritualism and magic, there are no owners nor prohibitive boundaries.

We will speak more about how such a personal cult can be developed, what it might contain, when it would be deployed, and the periods of day, night, and month when this magical and spirit office will be performed. It is an important part of the work of becoming a fully empowered and deeply knowledgeable Witch.

The Mysteries of light and darkness also play a part in this work, and so the diurnal passage of the Sun, the monthly occurrences of the Moon, and the seasonal journey of the Sun all play a part. While the temple is the heart of this work, even if it is a temporary use of space, a selected location in the wilds of nature would be the soul of this work since the Witch student should find a place of refuge and contemplation amidst the less trammeled parts our natural worlds. Even a park or a campground could be used for such a retreat. Such an occasional pilgrimage is an important part of functioning as a Witch.

We will cover all these rites, ceremonies, and liturgical obligations later in this work, but this is one very important half of the work required to become a Witch in more than name or role in the community. For now, it is important to know that a Pagan culture acts as a background that makes the spiritual workings of Witchcraft deeply rooted, empowered by the earth itself, relevant to today's world, and profound. You have free reign to build that culture in whatever manner you choose.

Location: A Very Private Practice

The place where these rites, ceremonies, and magic will be performed within a private home is called a temple. This place can be a room temporarily made up to be a temple, where furniture is moved around and positioned to make an optimal volume of space available for the work. If you are fortunate, you might have a room dedicated to being a permanent temple. I owned a home that not only had a permanent temple with a fireplace but also had an outside grove. I considered myself to be quite fortunate, but I have not always been so lucky. If your temple is a temporary affair, then you can consider your whole home, whether a house, a duplex, or even an apartment, to be a sacred temple. If you don't have access to a natural uncultivated space on your property, then you will likely need to find a park or campground outside of the urban or suburban locales and into the country to satisfy the second requirement—having a natural place for a retreat and regeneration.

Temple space can be simple or complex, sparse, or cluttered, depending on what is available to you and your tastes and personal habits. Still, a temple, whether temporary or permanent, must have a few pieces of furniture to practice Witchcraft.

First, you will need a table whose height reaches near to your waist for the altar, a smaller table for a shrine, a chair, and a large pillow or sitting cushion. That's all that you need as far as furniture, and these four furnishings can be decorated with colorful cloth coverings, embroidery, and arrayed with the various tools, implements, and decorations that are used to practice Witchcraft. One important factor is that this temple space must be private and capable of being secluded in some manner, with either a door or a curtain.

The main altar is often placed against a wall in one of the four cardinal points, typically a wall with no windows. At whatever direction the main altar is set will establish the element foundation of the temple. The smaller table shrine is typically placed in the opposite position to the main altar along with the chair. The sitting cushion can occupy any point in the temple, but I usually use it when meditating and set it aside when not using it.

In addition to these four pieces of furniture, I usually have some way of marking the four cardinal directions, which I call the four watchtowers. These are where four candles are placed to mark the cardinal directions with lights. What I have done is place two of the four candles on the main altar and shrine and then use two tall candlesticks to take the other two points for the magic circle. At the present time, I have opted to use battery-operated candles that have a realistic flicker like a real flame set to the quarters, since I have had the unfortunate experience of dealing with open flames and temple fire hazards. Some folks use glass oil lamps with paraffin oil as a safety factor, and others will use seven or fourteen-day votive candles which are glass enclosed and more difficult to catch things on fire. The four lights are complemented by two additional lights on the main altar and the shrine.

The four cardinal point candles and the two altars function as the perimeter of the magic circle. The circle, which is the foundation for the creation of sacred space, is usually imagined as a blue line of energy forming a circle around the periphery of the temple. You could, if it is something that appeals to you, have a magic circle drawn or painted on the floor if you have a hardwood floor. Some have opted to use a decorated fabric circle to act as the magic circle. I have never bothered with this kind of artifice except when I was starting out, and then I painted an elaborate magic circle with a seven-pointed start in the center on tag board. It was quite beautiful but awkward to use and certainly difficult to store. An imagined circle is the most efficient way of working with this artifice since it challenges the operator's imagination to perceive something that is not physically there. An imaginary magic circle is easy to invoke and banish, especially if the temple area is temporary.

Four cardinal directions in the magic circle are typically associated with the four elements, although that relationship is not fixed, but is quite arbitrary. For our purposes, we can ascribe a set of correspondences to the four cardinal points. These cardinal points are called watchtowers because they represent the protective focal points that guard or ward the sacred boundary of the magic circle that functions as the demarcation between the sacred and the profane. Outside of the circle is the material-based mundane world; within the circle is the sacred temple space where there is no time and all things spiritual and magical are possible. We call them watchtowers because it is believed that there is an entity or being which protects the quadrant of the temple. This being can be a lesser Deity, such as one of the four wind Gods, the elemental kings, the dread lords of the outer spaces (unnamed but possibly identified with the four demon chiefs), or even the four archangels. What you choose to use is completely your decision, since this is your own personal practice, guided by your own aesthetic choices. The four watchtowers can have many associations, and all these help to build up the qualities of archetypal symbols based on the number four. That number four symbolizes the basic powers available to the practicing Witch, and when combined with spirit, becomes the archetypal five-pointed star, or the pentagram.

Here is a table of these different watchtower correspondences for you to examine:

Direction	East	South	West	North
Element	Air	Fire	Water	Earth
Color	Yellow	Red	Blue	Green
Winds	Eurius	Notus	Zephyrus	Boreas
Totem	Raven	Cat	Toad	Goat

First Steps Toward Independent Witchcraft

Direction	East	South	West	North
Elementals	Paralda Sylphs	Djinn Salamanders	Nickasa Undines	Ghob Gnomes
Demon Chiefs	Oriens	Amaymon	Paimon	Ariton
Power	Mind	Will	Illusion	Change

These correspondences are arbitrary, which means that you can find sources where the attributions are different, depending on the traditional sources. However, all these associations can be found in various traditions, or they can be chosen or even made up. These are the four points that ward the magic circle, and the fifth point is in the center of the circle where all the forces combine into union. To activate these points, Witches use the device of the invoking pentagram and draw it to the four quarters. We will discuss this in greater detail when describing the ritual to consecrate the magic circle.

As I stated previously, the temple can be sparse with only a few decorations, or it can be elaborate and made into a permanent place of magic and a fit dwelling place for your Deities, ancestors, and spiritual allies. It will have some kind of illumination for the shrine at all times of the day, and it will smell of the herbs and incense burnt as offerings to Deities and spirits who will have place markers in that room. For this reason, it is important to either hide away these embellishments in a temporary temple or to keep the room sequestered and even locked so that unauthorized folk will not have entry if the temple is permanent.

Acquiring the Accouterments of the Craft

Every trade has its tools, and Witchcraft is no different. Magical tools can come in a variety of functional uses and styles, as is evident from the Solomonic grimoires from the previous age. However, the standard set of tools corresponds to the four elements, similarly to the four cardinal directions. The four elemental tools were taken from the Golden Dawn, and prior to that, it was likely that the tools that Witches used in the previous age were unadorned and functional, representing what was at hand to the typical rural resident. However, it is a convenient way to classify the four tools with the four elements, since that is also a convenient way to divide the work that a Witch will perform into four specific categories.

Here are the four tools, their element, and their function as used in modern Witchcraft. I have included a fifth because five is the number of Witches and it is best to always include spirit with the four elements.

Tool	Element	Function	Magic
Dagger or Athame	Air	Draw lines of force	Power of Division/Definition
Wand	Fire	Invoke spirits	Power of Summoning
Chalice or Cauldron	Water	Hold liquid sacraments	Sacramental Brewing
Pentacle	Earth	Hold solid sacraments	Sacramental Transformation
Stone or Crystal	Spirit	Collector	Magical Battery

The dagger or athame is the principal tool used for drawing lines of force or devices in the air. It is considered a weapon, so it is employed as a means of protecting a Witch against spiritual entities or forces. The dagger is the more personalized bladed weapon used by a Witch, whereas the sword represents the same tool qualities only in a greater level of power and authority. A sword is optional for a beginner Witch, while the dagger is essential. As a magical tool, it is consecrated and therefore not used for mundane purposes. I typically keep my dagger dull so that its use will in no way be a hazard, especially if I work with other Witches.

A Witch will often have a pair of knives to use, one with a black handle and the other, with a white handle. The black-handled knife or dagger will be the one that is consecrated for magical use, and it can also have magical symbols painted or etched on the handle. It is never used for mundane purposes. The white-hilted knife is the utility cutting tool that is used in the temple and can be used for all mundane and functional purposes.

TRADITIONAL ATHAME SIGILS

The wand is also an important tool, and where the dagger represents forcefulness, the wand is gentler but no less compelling, so it is used as an instrument to aid in the summoning and invoking of spirits, including the Deities. It is deployed like the dagger, but by drawing spirals in the air for invoking or banishing.

A wand is typically made of wood, and it should measure from the palm of your hand to the crook of your elbow. It can have a phallic tip or a rounded narrow point. It can be painted and adorned with magical symbols or kept plain. You can either construct your wand using your woodworking skills or purchase one from a store. This tool is also consecrated, so its use is reserved for sacred work. Like the sword, a larger version of the wand is the staff, which is an optional tool. A staff has the same qualities as a wand, except amplified, and it is also a sign of the authority and power of the Witch.

WAND SIGILS

The chalice or cauldron is an important tool because it is used to contain, brew, or hold sacramental offerings, particularly those that are liquid. A Witch will typically have both a chalice or cup and a cauldron since they are used for different purposes. A chalice is used to hold the lustral water or communion wine, but it can be used to make a liquid offering to an ancestral spirit, spiritual ally, or Deity. A cauldron has many functions and can be used in several different ways. It can be used to brew a drink, cook a potion or a stew, hold a food offering, or be used to burn a sigil parchment or aromatic herbs. It can also be used for divination if filled with water, allowing the operator to peer into its depths to enable scrying.

A chalice is made of metal so that it is durable, and often it is constructed of sterling silver or ceramic materials. I always have two chalices to separate the making of lustral water (salt and water) from the container of wine or ale offerings for communion. My lustral water chalice is made from ceramic and my communion chalice is made of silver. Both chalices occupy my main altar. My cauldron is set at the base of my main altar and can be taken wherever it is needed. A cauldron is made of a very durable material, typically iron or steel, and painted black. They come in many shapes and sizes and depending on their use, you will select one that fits your needs.

The pentacle is a dish that is inscribed with a pentagram. It is also a sacramental tool used to hold the solid offerings to spirits or the communion food, such as salt or bread. Like the chalice, I have two pentacles, one used to hold the salt and the other used for bread or food offerings. The pentacle can also be held by the edge when not holding sacraments and shown to the four quarters as a method for projecting sacramental powers throughout the temple.

A pentacle can be made of metal or ceramic. I have used pentacles that were made of copper or silver for the food sacraments and one that is ceramic for the salt. When not in use, I place the chalice on top of and resting on the pentacle, so I have the chalices for lustral water and wine placed on the altar residing on their respective pentacles. These are sacramental tools, so they can be grouped together.

The rock or crystal represents the foundation of the Witches' temple and the place where all energies are collected from each rite or ceremony that is performed in that space. In addition to storing this energy, it can also emanate certain called energies when a wand is used to siphon them from the crystal. This kind of operation can be performed only by someone who has developed the ability to see the energy fields and lines of force produced in a magic temple. Typically, I use a fist-sized crystal rock that has several crystal terminals to function as my foundation and spiritual touchstone.

All these tools are consecrated in a special ceremony that charges and sets them apart from mundane use. We will cover this specific rite later in this work. However, if you do not have the tools or know how to build your own tools, you can purchase them from various stores and vendors with the knowledge that they will be charged and altered when they are consecrated.

In addition, there will be other items that you will purchase, create, or find that will become a part of your temple equipment. You will need a container to burn incense, such as a thurible or censor that you can carry around the temple to spread the incense smoke to the four directions. The thurible does not need to be consecrated, since it will be sequestered by its use in the temple. Another item is the incense boat or container for the powdered incense, and an incense holder for a burning stick of incense. You will need incense, both powdered and stick, distilled water, coarse ground salt, wine or ale, bread, or cakes, and self-igniting charcoal briquettes for the thurible. Candles of different sorts along with candle sticks, seven or fourteen-day votive candles, and smaller votive candles for the shrine.

These are the basic collection of tools and supplies that you will need to use in your magical and religious work. Most of these can be found either in local stores, occult, Pagan, and New Age bookstores, or through online catalogs.

Preparations for the Work

Once you have furnished your designated sacred space, decorated it to your tastes, and collected the tools and supplies needed for the work, then you can work on the next and final beginning step and that is the adornment and preparations for yourself. It doesn't matter how fancy and fascinating your sacred space looks if you have not also prepared yourself for the work. This is the fun task of making yourself into a proper Witch practitioner. Since this work is going to be done in your private sacred space, then the only rules you need to follow are those that you feel are important.

Clothes do make the person, as the old saying goes, but what would you wear to work your own private version of Witchcraft? Traditional Witchcraft often stipulates that sacral nudity is a requirement, so the coven is required to perform their worship and magic nude, or *skyclad* as they call it. Gardnerian Witches nearly always follow this rule, but Alexandrians were more flexible. My perspective is that sacral nudity is not required unless someone is intimately engaged with worship of the Witchcraft Deities. When confronting the Deities, there must be nothing between them and us, which requires that we be as naked as when we were born. However, that kind of worship is not often needed, so when you are nude, it represents a special moment between you and the Gods. I use sacral nudity when performing a dedication rite to the Gods, but otherwise, I work robed.

What I have found is that wearing a robe that is comfortable is more important than wearing one that is overly decorative. If I am going to be spending hours wearing a robe, I would like it to be comfortable to wear. Not too warm and not too cold is probably an important consideration for the work. I also prefer wearing a black robe, but that is just my taste, since whatever color robe one wears should represent a personal statement. The same is true for jewelry, which can be simple or complex, based on individual tastes. My preference is for simplicity since I don't want my jewelry interfering with movement or ritual activities. I typically wear a necklace and maybe a ring—that is all I need to identify myself and my magic. I will let the choices for personal adornment be completely up to you, and experience over time will eliminate anything that is too ostentatious or awkward.

Preparation for magical or liturgical work requires that the practitioner be in the correct mental state, eager and willing to perform the work, and that they have performed some basic ablutions to be purified. What that means is that some kind of magical bath should be undertaken for anything more than a meditation session. It is particularly recommended if you are giving offerings and engaging with your chosen Deities. A bath or a shower is a good start, then followed with an anointing of perfumed oils on the forehead, hands, heart, above the genitals, and then the tops of the feet. A bath can be infused with herbs and oils, and a period of meditative soaking is often a good practice.

Some folks will spend a bit of time in front of a mirror once anointed and garbed to gaze into their reflection's eyes and practice a form of affirmation. Makeup can be applied to get the proper look, or not. I prefer to be plain, but you might wish to make yourself assume a more exotic look. Once again, this is based on your tastes and sense of aesthetics. I typically use the softer light of candles to create the proper ambiance for this task of ablutions and purification. Once these tasks are completed and you feel ready to engage in the work, you can proceed to the temple where you will light the candles, ignite the charcoal, light some incense sticks, and begin the work.

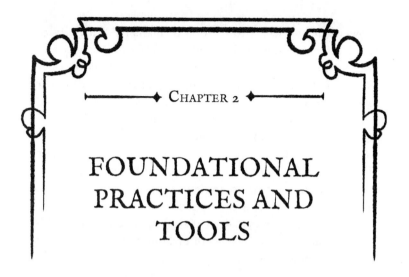

CHAPTER 2

FOUNDATIONAL PRACTICES AND TOOLS

Now that a proper space and all the tools and supplies for working Witchcraft have been assembled, and the robe and preparations collected and noted, the first step to be taken is to determine what a beginning Witch does after completing these preliminary steps. You have the supplies, the temple, a proper perspective, robes, jewelry, oils, incense, candles, and other important tools, and now you need to know what to do with them. I would guess that to be the million-dollar question. Now that you have it all, what do you do with it?

Foundational practices are the truly basic practices that are performed in the sacred space of a temple, which is another basic practice. While someone who is participating in a traditional coven or group knows all too well these basic practices, the solitary Witch might not have them all mastered. Still, even a traditional Witch might not have the complete set, so this is why we are going to cover them here in this chapter.

These practices teach a Witch how to meditate, adopt a trance state, use tools, navigate around a temple, make sacred space, write hymns and invocations to the selected Deities, develop a lunar and solar calendar and how to use it, and how, when, and where to perform divination. All these basic practices will need to be fully understood and automatic before we get to the more substantive workings, such as religious liturgy and magical workings. Some of these practices might seem intuitively obvious, but there is always a greater depth to even the simplest action, and covering these techniques is an important first step to more complex practices.

We begin this examination by looking at the various simple methods used for meditation and trance. These two practices are a critical keystone to the entire practice of Witchcraft. If you cannot perform the various methods of meditation, concentration, contemplation, visualization, and trance with the accompanying techniques of breathing, then you will not be able to reflexively control your conscious mind and direct your mental focus on anything. Self-directed mental control is a fundamental practice, so we should examine it thoroughly.

Meditation and Trance

Focusing the mind and controlling the breath are the two basic techniques that cover the fundamental methodology of meditation and trance. Movement and breath control are the techniques of manipulating energy within the body to produce a manifestation of magical power. However, the mind must be tackled first and foremost to produce the proper state of consciousness needed for most forms of liturgical and magical work. Still, in all these endeavors, controlling the breath is key to mastering them all.

DURATION SITTING: Most important in any kind of meditation is to be seated comfortably for the duration of the session. Some folks are quite comfortable sitting cross-legged with the back straight on a hard cushion that raises one's posterior several inches from the floor, allowing the legs to cross without cutting off the circulation of blood. Others may have issues with sitting cross-legged on the floor with or without a cushion, so for them, a chair is suitable. It is important to find a cushion[1] or a chair that can be sat upon for anywhere from several minutes to an hour. This is the first step to be followed in meditation.

As for breathing, we unconsciously inhale and exhale in a variable cycle at every moment of our existence. This happens, and we are mostly unaware of it happening. We breathe harder and our breathing cycle is shorter when we exert ourselves, and the cycle of our breathing is slow and regular when we sleep. Yet, to become aware of each inhalation and exhalation represents a different kind of bodily awareness, one that is fundamental to being consciously alive. If we take that awareness one step further, then we will breathe in a controlled manner, ensuring that our breathing cycle will be timed for inhalation and exhalation. There are many variations that can be adopted, but here is the basic pattern, known as the four-fold breath.

SIMPLE MEDITATION: While seated comfortably, become aware of your breathing cycle, and allow yourself to completely relax. Try to focus on your breathing and nothing else. Then, begin to count internally so that your inhalation will occur leisurely for four counts. Hold the breath in for four counts, then gently exhale to the count of four, and hold the breath with the lungs empty for the count of four. The trick is to make the counting slow and easy and to fully relax while timing breaths. Try to focus on your breathing. Let any extraneous thoughts come and go, paying them little attention. You can perform this four-fold breathing exercise anytime and anywhere, but to meditate in your temple has a special value and meaning. You can perform this exercise with your eyes open or closed.

---

[1] I would recommend a zafu and zabuton combination for meditation if you can manage sitting without back support.

SIMPLE TRANCE: Using the four-fold breath count to get to a meditative state, continue the structured breathing, using the counting activity. Focus your eyes on a particular object and stare at it, allowing yourself to blink occasionally, but keep the focus of your vision on that object. Try using a lit stick of incense or a candle. After a short period of time, you will notice a shift in your consciousness and the image will become slightly blurred and sometimes it will disappear. In this state of mind, you have entered a trance state. You can close your eyes and deepen this state, ignoring everything in your mind except the vision of that object you were staring at. Let it take you deeper and deeper, as your trance state develops. To resurface, willfully break your concentrated focus and allow yourself to become aware of the environment. Trance states are used to set the mood of a working and are employed before starting any kind of working.

COOL BREATHING: Since breath control is the key to moving energy through the body, then how that breath is controlled while the body is in movement is important for gathering and projecting energy from the body. Restricting the breath by drawing it through the mouth with the opening of the lips flattened so that it makes a hissing sound during inhalation or exhalation is the trick to what is called cool breathing. Cool breathing accompanies an action, such as pointing a dagger or wand, drawing a device, laying lines of force, or making spirals in the air. It is used to emphasize the projection of energy, such as when drawing a pentagram in the air and projecting a force into its center as a final flourish in drawing it. Cool breathing emphasizes a magical action, making it more dramatic but also projecting focused energy from the body.

BELLOWS BREATH: Taking breath control to its penultimate level is the bellows breath, a method of hyperventilation. Bellows breath is like panting, except that it is done with the mouth fully open with no restrictions, and the inhalation and exhalation

Foundational Practices and Tools

are performed quickly and forcefully. If done for a short period of time, typically for just several breaths, then it will charge the body with energy as a preparation for projecting it outwards using the cool breathing technique, where the aperture of the mouth closes during a forced exhalation, thereby projecting the energy out from the body into the object identified by the hand or hands pointing to it. When the bellows breath is done for a longer period, then it will cause a mild vertigo, and at that moment it should be stopped.

Induced Ecstasy: When you need to achieve a very deep trance state after an explosion of energy, typically done at the climax of a ritual working, you can use the combination of the bellows breath and body locking to produce a powerful explosion of energy and a deep trance aftermath. This is done by performing the bellows breath to the point of vertigo and then holding in the last breath, wrapping the arms around your body and both attempting to force the breath out and simultaneously holding it in. At the last moment, let the breath out explosively. You will likely see lights and experience your body vibrating with the flow of blood as your heartbeat drops down to a deep restful level. Allow yourself to assume a deep and restful meditative state for as long as it lasts. I have used this technique, although sparingly since it might possibly be a health risk if performed too frequently. While performing the bellows breath, you can also inhale a perfumed oil to cap off the experience.

Meditation Session: Using the four-fold breath technique, establish a deep and relaxing meditative state. Then once that state is achieved, you can stop counting but continue with the structured breathing. Focus on your breathing but allow yourself to observe any extraneous thoughts or feelings. Try not to engage with these thoughts and feelings or allow them to break your focus on your breathing. Simply observe these thoughts and feelings and then ignore them, allowing them to recede in your mind. Do this exercise at least once a day, every day, for at least twenty minutes. After several weeks, lengthen the time to thirty or forty minutes. While this might seem like a simple exercise, it is quite difficult to maintain, and even more difficult to ensure that you practice it regularly. This is a basic exercise, and you should be able to automatically adopt this meditation session whenever or wherever it is required.

VISUALIZATION: Visualization is a very powerful magical tool, and along with meditation, it should be developed so that you can visualize magical energies, mythical places superimposed over normal reality, or even transform the nature of what you are perceiving. Still, visualization begins with the simple steps of using your imagination while in a meditative state. You can record a visualization session or purchase one, but perhaps the optimal use of guided visualization is what I call the self-scan. This is where the mind is focused on each body part in succession, starting with the feet, visualizing that part, placing it into a relaxed and stress-free state, and then proceeding slowly up the body to the head. A self-scan is used to relax the body and to focus on parts of it that are experiencing pain or discomfort as a form of temporary relief. Other forms of visualization can be taking a trip into a mythical place while in deep meditation using a pre-recorded visualization exercise. We will cover this technique when we discuss the liturgical and magical workings since this technique is used to make such workings more actualized.

CONCENTRATION: Concentration is an exercise that teaches you to be able to focus your attention on an object without allowing any intervening thoughts or feelings to cause that focus to be broken. Concentration is a simple but extremely difficult exercise. You need to focus on something that is in movement, like the second hand on a watch, or a timer countdown on a cell phone. Your objective is to focus

Foundational Practices and Tools

on this moving object without any thoughts or feelings causing a break for at least five minutes. That task will be quite daunting, and a successful conclusion will likely elude you for some time. However, over a period, you should be able to master this task for just five minutes, and when that happens, increase the time to seven minutes. Perform this exercise as an add-on to your daily meditation session, especially right after you have completed it.

CONTEMPLATION: Contemplation can be defined in two ways. It is used in conjunction with a meditative state to either focus on emptiness, or it is used to focus on a concept, issue, or tenet of belief while carefully observing, in a detached manner, all the thoughts and feelings that it evokes. It is easier and more instructive to contemplate concepts, issues, or tenets than to focus on emptiness. This type of meditation is quite useful to track down mental associations and feelings that are aligned to a specific subject. I often use this technique to track down the sources of personal issues or situations that troubled or disturbed me. The idea is to be completely detached and observe how your mind reacts to a given subject. You can also use this technique to further your understanding of an opinion or a belief that you have believed in which has turned out to be inaccurate or incorrect. Contemplation is used during a meditative session that is performed before a specific magical ritual is to be performed, assisting the operator in knowing and understanding mental associations and feelings before the work commences.

These practices are the basic techniques of personal mental control that are used in both the religious exercises and magical workings as practiced in modern Witchcraft. I would recommend that you practice them as often as you can until they become an automatic behavior that can be used whenever needed.

Four Elemental Tools and Their Use

We have already covered the four elemental tools in the previous chapter. However, what we haven't touched on is how they are used and what purpose they serve. This, of course, is important so that when these tools are used in the rituals, you will understand what they are used for and how to use them, and that will make the ritual itself more accessible. You can think of elemental tools as possessing attributes associated with the element to which they are assigned. All these tools, whether consecrated by rite or use, are to be set aside once they are dedicated to the Craft.

Dagger or Athame
Element: Air

The element of Air is symbolized by the activity of the mind and its ability to name, associate, and categorize. The dagger is used to draw lines of force in sacred space, which can divide or connect objects, or determine shapes. It is used to draw the boundary of the magic circle, to charge and bless the water and salt, wine, and bread, transforming them into sacraments. It is a consecrated tool, and the operator wields it using the cool breath to push magical energy through the body into the tool and beyond it. Visualizing the lines of force produced by the dagger is very helpful to perceive its function.

Wand
Element: Fire

The element of Fire is symbolized by physical action, consumption, power, authority, and as a torch, light. The wand is used like the dagger, except that it is more of a symbol of authority than an instrument of power. It is used to invoke and summon spirits and even Deities and to give them license to depart. The operator uses it to draw invoking and banishing spirals to draw in and send out spiritual entities. I also use the wand to draw devices such as the cross, ankh, or any other device that functions as a symbol of Deity. Like the dagger, the spirals or devices should be perceived through visualization. The wand is also a consecrated tool.

Chalice or Cauldron
Element: Water

The element of Water is symbolized by the emotions and internal psychic processes, such as dreams, visions, or portends. The chalice is used to contain liquid sacraments, such as lustral water or wine. Its utility is that it is a container, and like all containers, resonates with the symbolic characteristics of the feminine archetype and its corollary life-giving female Deities. The cauldron has a wider range of uses since it can be used to brew, cook, select by lot, burn parchment, or used to scry when filled with water. Like the chalice, it is important to keep the cauldron clean and ready for use. The chalice and the cauldron are not consecrated; instead, they are charged and blessed through constant use.

Pentacle
Element: Earth

The element of Earth is characterized by the physical body, material things, life, flora and fauna, vital force, mortality, change, creativity, and fertility. The pentacle is used to hold solid sacraments, such as bread, cakes, or salt. As both a tool and a symbol of the earth itself (a pentagram), it is the foundation point where material objects are sacralized by the powers of spirit and earth joined. It can be used as a plate to hold items and it can also be used to project the energies of the element of earth when held like a mirror and aimed throughout the magic circle. The pentacle is not consecrated. Since it has a pentagram inscribed on it, simple use will activate its powers.

Other Tools

The other tools that are used in a temple can have a loose association with the elements and would not have to be consecrated by a rite. The thurible or censor would be associated with the element of Air, and the operator would either swing it on its chain or carry it to the places in the circle that required to be incensed. The candles are, of course, associated with the element Fire, and so would lamps or even battery-operated luminary candles. Other element attributes would be loosely associated with powdered incense (Earth), wine (Water), bread (Earth), charcoal briquettes (Fire), etc. Only the censor and candles have any kind of regular association with an element.

Magic Circle, Altar, and Shrine

The three furniture components of a temple are the main altar, the shrine, and the four markers or candles for the four watchtowers. The temple is decorated in whatever manner suits your sense of aesthetics, but it is important to further discuss the temple and its essential magical topology.

A temple is not only a furnished space, but it is also an archetypal world within a world. Once consecrated for a working, a temple assumes a sacred space that is filled with spiritual and mythological meaning and represents a meeting place between the domain of Deities and the material world of humanity. A consecrated circle is an in-between place that stands as a lintel between two worlds, and as such, it is a place of magic and spirits. In sacred space, there is no time except the present, and what is in the past and the future are collapsed into a single dimension of consciousness. Making sacred space is the whole purpose for the furniture of the temple.

In the art of Witchcraft, a magic circle does not function as it would in the workings of a ceremonial magician and their rites. A ceremonial magician uses the magic circle as a ring or boundary of protection that keeps potentially hostile or neutral spirits from possessing or harming them. A Witches' circle is completely the opposite, acting as a boundary to determine the distinction between the sacred and the profane. Instead of protecting the inhabitants from spiritual contagion, a Witch uses their circle to contain all that is spiritual so they might commune directly with it in the sacred precincts of a temple of the Gods.

There are no internal boundaries in a magic circle and temple consecrated by a Witch. They are exposed to everything in that spiritual domain, using their alignment to the Deities of their elected pantheon to mitigate and protect them from inimical spirits or other Deities. Their space is safe because it is dedicated to their Deities, and that trust is given to make their sacred space safe and inviolate.

What is important for a Witch is that the attributes of the profane world be kept out of their sacred space, and that is the function of the watchtowers and the pentagram wards that they set for them. They also will keep their workings secret and the place where they do this work secured from the attentions of those not aligned or initiated into their path.

The altar will typically hold the working tools of chalices, wand, and dagger, the two altar lights, and the central watchtower light for the cardinal direction. Other tools placed there would be the thurible or censor, incense boat, and a book holder for the personal Book of Shadows. Sacraments can be poured and placed in their receptacles, along with the charcoal in the censor, if there is to be a working, but otherwise, the other supplies would be stored in convenient locations.

Across from the main altar is the shrine, which is a smaller altar used to hold the artifacts and representations of the Deities, ancestors, and spiritual allies that a Witch will accumulate over time. The shrine is also the place where votive offerings are given and received and is the focus for such liturgical rites. There are no tools placed on a shrine since anything that is placed there belongs wholly to the Deities and cannot be used by humans except to worship them.

Four watchtowers represent the periphery of the magic circle and the sacred space of the temple. They reside at the boundary between the sacred precincts of the temple and the outer world of the profane. The watchtowers are the residence of various spirits invoked to protect and guard the circle from the outer world. These spirits are called sequentially when the circle is consecrated, and the watchtower is warded or set with an invoking pentagram to the specific elemental associated with the cardinal direction.

In addition to the four watchtowers marking the four cardinal points, there are three points in the center of the circle. Standing in the center of the circle reveals these three points. The first is above you, the second is below your feet, and the third is the midpoint represented by your heart. These three points are named the zenith, nadir, and mid-point, respectively. These three points and the four cardinal directions in the ring of the circle characterize the sacred space as occupying a sphere that is placed above the ceiling and below the floor of the temple. When the circle is consecrated and an energy charge is generated in that space, it will appear as a sphere of subtle luminous energy.

Once established, the magic circle is treated as a boundary that is not to be crossed unless one needs to for various reasons. If you must leave a magic circle or let someone in, then the dagger would be used to draw a door in the circle, and the person entering or exiting would turn in a clockwise spiral as they entered or exited. The door is left open so one can return, and it is closed when someone fully enters or returns to this space, using the dagger to draw an "X" over the doorway and then erase it with the hand holding the dagger. Visualizing this as it is occurring will help you to experience it fully.

Movement in the magic circle has significance, so you should be aware which direction you are moving in a consecrated magic circle. You can move directly from one point to another, for instance, walking from the eastern watchtower to the western watchtower, but most movements are circular instead of direct, and they move in either a deosil (clockwise) or widdershins (anti-clockwise) direction. Deosil is a movement with the Sun, and it represents the winding up of energy and is the path of light because of that association. Widdershins is the movement against the Sun, and it represents the loosening or releasing of energy and is the path of darkness.

There are two spiral movements in the circle, where the operator walks from the outer periphery of the circle to its center or walks from the center to the outer periphery of the circle. The first spiral inward concentrates the energy in the circle in the center and the second spiral causes the energy to be loosened or exteriorized, exiting where the operator points and projects the energy beyond the circle boundary. Cool breathing is used to wind the power and concentrate it in the center, and bellows breathing is used to exteriorize the energy, especially when the energy is projected out of the circle.

Now that we have covered the temple, circle, and its various attributes and their use, we can move on to the very important ritual of circle consecration, which makes sacred space in the temple. Sacred space is the domain where all liturgical operations occur and where magical energy is generated, concentrated, and unleashed.

Circle Consecration Rite: Making Sacred Space

All Witchcraft operations are performed in sacred space, including more extensive meditations, divination, regular votive offerings, magical spell work, and liturgical workings. Since this is the foundational state in which most operations are performed, it should be given and explained very early in the exposition of Witchcraft activity. When I teach people to function as Witches, one of the first rituals that I teach is the circle consecration. It is the starting point for all other endeavors, so it should be learned and mastered thoroughly.

The circle consecration ritual is fundamental to Witchcraft work, so it can be deployed in several manners. It can be a simple rite without much dialogue, or it can be elaborate. It should be formulated in such a way that it can be easily memorized, and there can be different versions of the same rite to be used in one's set of ritual tools. I have several elaborately scripted circle consecration rites and then I have a simple version that I have memorized to use when I need to make sacred space quickly and efficiently. What I am going to present here is more of the latter type of circle consecration rite, since that should be the one that you develop and fully memorize.

Basically, the circle consecration rite has four levels or parts to it. The first part is the making of the lustral water, which is charging the salt and charging and blessing the water, and then mixing them together to create the sacrament of the lustral water.[2] Lustral water is like the holy water that the Catholic church uses, except that it has a greater content of salt, making it more like the brine of the sea or amniotic fluid. It is the liquid associated with life, and so as a sacrament, it symbolizes the sacred polarized joining of Water and Earth (the joining of the archetypal feminine and masculine).

The second part is where the sacred space is blessed by the four elements of lustral water (Earth and Water), incense smoke, and candlelight. The third part is where the operator draws the magic circle using the dagger over the sanctified floor of the temple, joining the watchtowers in a ring of power as projected by the dagger.

The fourth part of the ritual is where the operator summons the demigod associated with the cardinal direction and then sets the ward by drawing an invoking pentagram to the element of the watchtower. This is done starting in the east and proceeding around the circle to the south, west, and north. This progression is a deosil circle that proceeds from the element of Air to the element of Earth, which is also the arc of manifestation.

Let us now proceed with a description of this ritual.

---

[2] Salt is already considered to be blessed, so it is just charged. Water must be blessed and charged.

Ritual for Circle Consecration

The operator performs a meditation session lasting for twenty minutes before proceeding with the rite. The temple is prepared for work but is dimly lit. The operator lights the watchtower candles and then the candles for the main altar and the shrine. They light the self-igniting charcoal and then wait a brief time for all to be ready. They have ensured that the chalice of water is near enough to use. They will perform this rite in the name of Deities which are their primary pantheon, replacing their name for the X.

Before the main altar, they take up the dagger, holding it with both hands, slowly plunge it into the chalice of water, and then say:

"I bless and charge this water in the name of X."

They remove the chalice from the pentacle where the salt is exposed. They hold the dagger in both hands and slowly plunge it into the salt and say:

"I charge this salt in the name of X."

Then they take the dish of salt and turn it so that it pours into the water, put down the dish, and place the chalice back upon it. They take the dagger in both hands and slowly plunge it into the mixture of salt and water, saying:

"Salt and water joined together makes this water of life, in the name of X."

The operator takes the chalice and proceeds to the eastern watchtower, holding it in their left hand. While dipping the fingers of their right hand into the chalice, they sprinkle drops of the lustral water before them, doing this as they proceed from the east to the south, west, and then in the north, continuing until they reach the east again.

The operator returns to the altar and sets the chalice on the pentacle. Using a spoon, the operator scoops a small amount of powdered incense onto the ignited charcoal and then replaces the spoon, drops the cover on the censer, and then takes it up with its chain, proceeding to the eastern watchtower. Once there, they incense the watchtower and proceed deosil to the south, west, north, and return to the east, having dispensed incense smoke to all the four quarters. They return the censer to the altar.

They take up one of the altar candles in their left hand and proceed to the eastern watchtower, where they lift and lower the candle stick, and then move it side to side to form an equal arm cross. They then proceed deosil to the south, west, and north, and return to the east, performing the same operation.

They return to the altar, place the altar candle on the altar and then take up the dagger. They proceed to the eastern watchtower and stand before it. Then pointing down to where the floor meets the wall, they begin to draw a line of power from that point and proceed deosil to the south, then the west, north, and finally, return to the east. As they are drawing this line of force, they perform cool breathing and visualize a line of blue energy projecting from the dagger to the ring that is being drawn.

Having returned to the east, they stand momentarily before it. Holding the dagger aloft and pointing at the imagined watchtower, they say the following.

> *"I summon and call you, Oh Dread Lord of the East, whose emissary is Eurius, the Eastern Wind, to protect and ward this temple."*

They then draw an invoking pentagram of Air into the watchtower and point their dagger into its center and exhale their energy into it.[3]

---

3   Method used to draw pentagrams is covered in Chapter Four.

Foundational Practices and Tools

They proceed to the south and stand momentarily before it. Holding the dagger aloft, they say:

"I summon and call you, Oh Dread Lord of the South, whose emissary is Notus, the Southern Wind, to protect and ward this temple."

They draw an invoking pentagram of Fire into the watchtower and point their dagger into its center and exhale their energy into it.

The operator proceeds to the west and stands momentarily before it. Holding the dagger aloft, they say:

"I summon and call you, Oh Dread Lord of the West, whose emissary is Zephyrus, the Western Wind, to protect and ward this temple."

They draw an invoking pentagram of Water into the watchtower and point their dagger into its center and exhale their energy into it.

They proceed to the north and stand momentarily before it. Holding the dagger aloft, they say:

"I summon and call you, Oh Dread Lord of the North, whose emissary is Boreas, the Northern Wind, to protect and ward this temple."

They draw an invoking pentagram of Earth into the watchtower and point their dagger into its center and exhale their energy into it.

Then the operator returns to the altar and places the dagger on it, bows their head, and says:

"This sacred circle is now set, and let all spiritual and magical things safely occur within it. The rite is completed."

To banish a circle that has been set, the operator only needs to begin at the eastern watchtower, drawing a banishing pentagram of Air,[4] and then give the spirit of the watchtower license to depart in peace. They will perform this banishing pentagram at each of the other three watchtowers for the associated element and give the spirit of the watchtower the license to depart. After these actions, they should extinguish the altar candles, the shrine candles, and finally, the watchtower candles.

Building a Lunar and Solar Calendar

It is important to state that rituals must not only be learned to be executed properly, but they must also be performed at the right time. A Witch performs their rites to the ever-changing clock of the diurnal cycle of day and night, but also the cycle of the Moon and the seasons of the Sun. Magical operations are performed in accordance with the cycle of the Moon, where the full moon is considered the most auspicious time. Liturgical rites are performed in accordance with both the lunar and solar cycles. The lunar esbat is both a magical and liturgical operation, and the sabbat is mostly a liturgical celebration. It is important to mark these dates on a calendar and have the means to quickly know in what phase the Moon resides for any planned or unplanned working.

Lunar phases occur over the course of a single month, and the full moon can occur at any point in the month during its twenty-eight-day cycle through the zodiac. While the full moon would be reserved for the Witches' esbat rite, the other phases would represent different kinds of energy that could be used in either magical or divinatory workings. The qualities of the four basic phases of the Moon, for the new moon,

---

4   Banishing pentagram drawing directions are found in Chapter Four.

first quarter, full, and last quarter are comparable to the four elements, and this helps to distinguish those qualities.

The elemental qualities that the four phases of the Moon have are:

- New Moon: Earth
- First Quarter: Air
- Full Moon: Fire
- Last Quarter: Water

The new moon is good for beginning new projects, such as in the old saying, "planting in the new moon ensures a full harvest." The first quarter is a time for activity and preparations—these are the days when magic is best performed. The full moon is where the lunar energies achieve their highest expression, so this is a good time to connect to the Deities and engage them in a final push to complete one's work. The last quarter is a good time for reflection and divination, a time to determine if the magic sent out earlier is doing the work that it should, which leads to the new moon that starts the whole cycle again.

The quality of the full moon has behind it an extensive folklore that can and should be used to qualify your full moon esbats. I assembled much of my full moon lore from the Farmer's Almanac.[5] There are a lot of other sources that can be found for this kind of lore since many Pagan publishing firms and online websites will have this kind of information you can use. I would recommend that you create your own Moon book to store this lore, so you can use it when planning a magical working. You should have a calendar that shows the phases of

---

5   Farmer's Almanac Editors, *Full Moon Calendar* at Farmer's Almanac, accessed December 31, 2021: https://www.farmersalmanac.com/full-moon-dates-and-times

the Moon, their dates, and times, which will help you to know when these events accurately occur.[6]

Eight sabbats occur in the Witches' Wheel of the Year, representing the Sun's journey through the zodiac each year. While these solar sabbats lack the dynamism of the lunar esbats, they clearly represent the play of light and darkness, life and death, that occurs through the year. There are two sets of sabbats.

The first set are called the quarter dates, and these are the solstices and equinoxes that represent the first day of the changing four seasons. These dates are points of transition in the quality of the light, but not in outward appearance of the season, so depending on where you are in the northern hemisphere, there will seem to be few signs of the season that has just begun. For instance, the spring equinox occurs roughly around March 21, yet in most places in the U.S., it will still seem a lot like winter. The autumn equinox still feels like summer, but the summer and winter solstice will seem a lot more like summer and winter. Each of these transition points occur when the Sun enters a cardinal zodiacal sign, such as Aries for spring equinox, Cancer for summer solstice, Libra for the autumn equinox, and Capricorn for winter solstice.

The second set of sabbats are called the cross-quarter dates, and these are the mid-point of the season and represent the forces of nature reaching their full expression for that season. As a cycle, these sabbats reflect more the state of life as they appear in nature than in terms of the degree of light and darkness. Cross-quarter sabbats represent the life cycle where the solstices and equinoxes represent the passage of the Sun and its apparent light upon the Earth. I have always seen these two sets of celebrations as distinct, even though they together represent the cycle of light and darkness of the Sun, life, and death of nature.

---

6   I would recommend purchasing an astrological calendar of some kind that shows the lunar phases during the month, and the exact times of the equinoxes and solstices, not to mention the other four cross quarter celebrations. One such calendar that I use is *Llewellyn's Daily Planetary Guide*.

Table of the Eight Sabbats

Event	Element	Sign	Quadruplicity	Quality
Spring Equinox	Fire	Aries	Cardinal	Rebirth of Life, Beginnings Executed
Beltane	Earth	Taurus	Fixed	Fertility, Growth, Material Happiness
Summer Solstice	Water	Cancer	Cardinal	Zenith of Light, Blessings of Life
Lammas	Fire	Leo	Fixed	Celebrations, First Harvests, Travel
Autumn Equinox	Air	Libra	Cardinal	Full Harvest, Thanksgiving, Preparations
Samhain	Water	Scorpio	Fixed	Opening Spirit Gates, Night of the Dead
Winter Solstice	Earth	Capricorn	Cardinal	Longest Night, Rebirth of Light
Candlemas Eve	Air	Aquarius	Fixed	Purification, Fasting, Celebration of Light

The table of the eight sabbats shows the element, zodiacal sign, quadruplicity, and quality that qualifies each of these celebrations. They have themes and lots of folklore that anyone can gather, and that folklore has a deeper meaning and significance that you might examine and research over time. Ultimately, the sabbats are solar Mysteries that are as deep and important magically as the lunar cycle and its Mysteries.

In my opinion and practice, the esbats are for engaging with the Mysteries and magic of the Moon, and the sabbats are for celebrating the seasonal milestones of the solar year. Since this book is about the private and independent practice of a Witch, I believe that there is no excuse for not doing some rite at exactly on the day that the season changes or achieves its midpoint, or the Moon becomes full.

A coven or a community often will schedule their esbats and sabbats so they are convenient to a group of people, and this means that the event will be scheduled on the weekend before or after the date if it occurs during the week. A private practice doesn't have such restrictions, so it is prudent to perform the rite on the exact date the lunar or solar event occurs. For magical workings, there is some period of days from the new moon to the full moon in which to perform the specific magic rite. Otherwise, obeying the calendar will be very beneficial for the independent Witch. It will synchronize their beings with the cycle of nature. While the coven or community will have to bend the rules to accommodate everyone, the independent Witch can perform their own rite and attend the coven or community event if desired.

As I stated, an esbat is for private Mysteries and magic, and can employ magical workings along with the obligatory liturgical rites. However, a sabbat is a different matter. If possible, it is always good to attend a community or the local coven gathering for these rites if one is a member. An independent Witch can also perform a simple liturgical operation on the exact day of the solar sabbat event to keep their calendrical exercises and works in continual engagement.

Foundational Practices and Tools

Developing Hymns and Invocations to the Deities

Once you have chosen a pantheon of Deities to act as your personal religious cult, you will need to develop and write three liturgical texts for each one. This is very important work, since these three texts will be used in your liturgical workings. Since I have declared that you should have a close engagement and alignment to a set of Deities with a cultural background of some type, these three texts for each Deity will be the starting point in developing that relationship.

These three texts are:

1. Description of the Deity's image, personality, and suitable offerings.
2. Hymn to the Deity: a short set of statements praising and giving thanks to the God or Goddess.
3. Invocation to the Deity: a short set of statements calling the God or Goddess to appear and bless and accept offerings given.

Other types of textual material would include any stories, myths, or folklore associated with this specific Deity, as well as songs, symbols, seals, or signs. Additionally, possessing any image or likeness of the Deity would represent an important placeholder or link to that Deity. Such a link can be placed on the shrine where it will be given the full attention associated with the Deity.

To develop these three texts, it will be important to do some research and gather this information from historical sources (if they exist) or current reconstructed religious practices, or to fill in what is not known by using your imagination. These three texts and anything else that is relevant will be put into your personal Book of Shadows to be used whenever you engage your Deities in rites and religious practices. I will give you some examples of what these might look like in the appendix for this book. I will discuss the various liturgical rites and the obligations of an independently practicing Witch in Chapter Three.

Divination Techniques

To determine the will of the Gods, you should have the means to perform divination, since this is exactly what the term divination means: seeking guidance and learning the desires of your personal Deities. While divination is often disconnected from the Deities that are a part of one's worship, and in fact, divination has become a secular affair with no reference to Deity, I believe that it is important to bring that focus back into practice. To give homage to the Gods before performing any divination, and then thanking them for their revelations afterward, will likely make the session more meaningful and the results clearer.

Where magic is the actions that a Witch will take to bend the laws of probability, it is divination that will show if the potential to achieve an objective is possible. Divination is the mechanism of knowing something without having direct access to it. You can divine the past, figure out the present, and determine the proper course for the future. Divination acts as the eyes and ears of the Witch, extending those senses beyond the normal boundaries to gain insights and an understanding of an otherwise complex and opaque world. Of all the systems of magic, divination is, in my opinion, the most important.

There are several divination tools available today, but for the beginner, this list can be pared down to the essential set of tools. Keep in mind that for each divination tool, you will need to perform a deep dive into researching and learning to use and master that tool. Each method of divination is a discipline, requiring a lot of time and effort to master, distinct from the other practices, both liturgical and magical.

Here are some examples of divination that I would recommend you learn and master. These methods will certainly add to your ability to determine the nature of the forces and conditions that are occurring beyond your ability to actively know. Some of these methods will be easy for you to master and others will be difficult or even impossible. It is important, however, to master at least two of these methods.

DICE OR KNUCKLE BONES: Simple yes or no, or more complex responses. This tool should be first and foremost the tool that you adopt and master.[7]

TAROT CARDS: Determine events, possibilities, or underlying conditions that might help or block a magical working.

ASTROLOGY: Defines the potential self (natal chart) and the potential events (transit, progression, or elective charts). This discipline takes some time to be merely competent.

GERMANIC RUNES OR GEOMANCY STICKS: Function as an oracle with a finite set of responses.

PENDULUM: Can determine locations or simple responses to questions—requires a map or response base.

CRYSTAL BALL, OBSIDIAN DISK, WATER SCRYING: Empowers a clairvoyant ability to see potential events or underlying conditions expressed in a symbolic or dreamlike vocabulary. This discipline is very difficult to adopt and requires certain psychic abilities most people lack.

Since I am suggesting that you should bring the Deities of your personal cult into the process of divination, then the best place to perform this work is in a consecrated circle. The exception,

---

[7] Frater Barrabbas, *Spirit Conjuring for Witches*, 183–185. This reference has a good explanation for a divination method using dice.

of course, is astrology. There are also some important rules to consider when performing divination.

- Ask clear questions that you don't know the answer to, and never repeat the same question during the same or recent session.
- Never take the results of a divination as an order or an obligation.
- Never perform a divination session when sick or indisposed.
- Be respectful and reverent when performing a session.
- Briefly ask the Deities for guidance and thank them afterward.
- Write down the questions and the results of the reading and keep them in your diary.
- For a strategic and important question, you can consider performing more than one divination session and using different divination systems for comparison.
- Whatever you decide to do after performing a session, keep in mind that it is your decision and that you have the free will to make an informed one.

CHAPTER 3

LITURGICAL PRACTICES PERFORMED IN SACRED SPACE

ONE-HALF OF THE WORK of an independent Witch is to engage with their Deities and establish a powerful alignment through various liturgical practices. They do this so that the Deities will help and aid them in their magical workings. Some of the magic in Witchcraft is sacramental in nature, and this can only occur through the agency of the Deities. The basic premise of this work is that Witches give worship to their Goddesses and Gods in the form of prayers, hymns, offerings, and invocations so that they can receive their power, authority, and blessings in the form of a spiritually and materially fulfilled existence.

Pagan Deities are seldom depicted as being alone or solitary, since their temples in the near and distant past have shown that they reside with other Deities and demigods, forming a close-knit family. This is the reason why I have always proposed that Witches have in their religious work a pantheon of related Goddesses and Gods, along with their associated heroes and heroines, and other mythical beings.

Still, it is also a good idea to forge a special relationship with one of these Deities who has a particular appeal and identification with the worshipper. This Deity will adopt a more singular and intimate representation as the Witch engages with it, thereby creating a strong alignment, and correspondingly, the Witch identifies with this being. That is the expected normal progression in the evolution of the liturgical obligations assumed by a Witch engaging in a personal and independent practice. Ultimately, such a relationship will allow for a regularly practiced godhead assumption and perhaps even a personification; but for the beginner, such an approach will not be required until that relationship deepens and matures over time.

Forging a relationship with a pantheon and with a specific Deity within that pantheon requires certain obligations on the part of the Witch. The adage, "If you want something from someone, then you have to do something for them," applies to this kind of relationship. It is a quid pro quo exchange between Deity and humanity, and one that is fundamental to Witchcraft practices that integrate religion and magic.

A Witch who is practicing their Craft alone will become both the officiant and the congregation of their own private and personal cult of the Gods. Their obligations fall only on their shoulders, and it is a responsibility that they cannot share or delegate. It is completely the sole responsibility of the Witch to develop a strong and unbreakable alignment with their Deities through the continual religious practices that they will develop and employ.

These practices consist of the following rites that the Witch will perform on a regularly occurring schedule. You should examine these rituals with the understanding that you will need to write, practice, and employ these rituals to fulfill your obligations and function as an independent Witch.

DAILY PRACTICES: Prayers, hymns, and meditations in sacred space focused on the pantheon and the specific favorite Deity. Basic religious meditative and prayer session.

Liturgical Practices Performed in Sacred Space

Weekly Practices: Votive offerings and religious service. Prayers, hymns, meditations, then invocations, and the giving of offerings to the Deities.

Monthly Practices: Votive offerings, communion, and full moon Mystery. Prayers, hymns, meditations, and invocations, followed by offerings to the Deities, then a request for blessings and communion. Meditation and contemplation on the specific qualities of the full moon.

Seasonal Practices: Votive offerings, communion, and seasonal solar Mystery. Prayers, hymns, meditations, and invocations, followed by offerings to the Deities, then a request for blessings and communion. Meditation and contemplation on the specific qualities of the seasonal sabbat.

These are the periodic practices that are required to build the proper relationship alignment with the elected Deities. While these practices are wielded together as a religious discipline, they represent the minimum requirement for the periodic liturgical rites and practices to be adopted by the independent Witch. As you can see, being solitary and independent requires a greater degree of work and effort than if one belongs to a coven and the leaders do this work for you. Still, the cost in labor might be high, but so are the rewards.

What I have found in following these practices over the years is that I find myself falling out of this discipline and having to restart it again. In the beginning, I performed these kinds of periodic rites faithfully for several years, but then life intervened and I found that I had to start over.

You should never feel that you have somehow failed if you begin this kind of discipline but can only follow it for a while. Like meditating where you break your focus and must refocus again, keeping a regimen of spiritual practices is likely impossible for most, so you will find yourself dropping out of this discipline and having to restart it after a while. That's expected, and even the most experienced practitioners must restart after an unplanned or unforeseen hiatus. The important consideration is that if you expect to perform a series of magical workings, it is best if you have also adopted a spiritual discipline prior to that time to empower them with the magic and Mystery of the Gods.

Now let us examine the rites and practices that establish the backbone of a Witchcraft practice.

Votive Offerings, Prayers, Meditation, Seasonal Practices

The first and most common practice in this suite of religious practices is the meditation and prayer session. This is the combination of a meditation session, previously discussed, and the additions of specific prayers and hymns to each of the Deities in the pantheon, with a special emphasis on the one Goddess or God that is to become the primary godhead amongst them. This session can be practiced in sacred space or outside it, at least once a day. Here is the pattern for that rite. You can use a chair instead of a cushion if your preferred sitting arrangement requires it for the sitting meditation.

1. Stand before the shrine and light some candles and a stick of incense to be affixed to the holder, and then back away and bow.
2. With arms and hands extended in an entreaty, recite a memorized short hymn or prayer to each of the Deities of the pantheon.
3. Sit on a cushion and perform the meditation session for twenty minutes.
4. Stand up, bow before the shrine, and address each Deity, thanking them for attending your prayer session. Extinguish the votive candles if they are not glass encased.

Liturgical Practices Performed in Sacred Space

The second practice is the weekly votive offering to the Deities, which is more elaborate than the meditation and prayer session, although it includes that in its practice as well. The votive offering is where the officiant will give offerings of light and incense to the Deities, using the thurible to fully incense the area of the shrine, and lighting all the offering candles.

This rite is performed in sacred space, so the circle will be consecrated before this work commences. In addition to the prayer hymns, the officiant will also use the image descriptions and the invocation calls to each Deity, asking them to descend and bless the temple. When this rite is performed as part of a full moon esbat or solar sabbat, the officiant will present to the Deities token offerings of food and drink. Here is the pattern for this rite.

1. Perform the circle consecration and any preparation steps required for a full temple operation.
2. Stand before the shrine and light some candles. Then using the thurible, incense the whole area of the shrine table. Then bow low before the shrine and back away from it, facing the shrine from a comfortable distance.
3. With arms and hands extended in an entreaty, recite a memorized short hymn or prayer to each of the Deities in the pantheon.
4. Kneel and bow before the shrine briefly touching the head to the floor, and then rise and recite the memorized invocation for each of the Deities, including the short description to formulate an image of each one.
5. If this is a monthly full moon or a solar sabbat, then the officiant will rise and proceed to the main altar to get the food and drink offering and place it on the shrine. Officiant bows low before the shrine and says:

I offer unto you a more fitting sacrifice of food and drink, given to you as a sign of my care, devotion, and alliance. May this offering please you and be acceptable.

6. Retrieve a cushion and sit upon it before the shrine and perform the meditation session for around fifteen minutes.
7. Stand up, bow before the shrine, and address each Deity, thanking them for attending your prayer session. If there is a magical working for either an esbat or a sabbat, then this step would be delayed until the magical operation was completed.

Once that rite is completed, then the officiant may continue with the work planned for that evening, or if there is no work, the meditation can be extended to thirty minutes or more. If your preferred seating is a chair instead of a cushion, then you can move the chair from next to the shrine to be situated in front of it when the meditation session is to be performed. When this rite is performed for a full moon esbat or a solar sabbat, then there will be an additional step added to contemplate the Mystery associated with that event. These two rites are used to cover the liturgical exercises to be performed daily and weekly, with additions for an esbat or a sabbat. Performing these rites every day and weekly will be the basic religious discipline for a Witch who seeks to build a private and personal approach to Witchcraft.

Full Moon Esbats

The full moon esbat is a religious and magical working, so it has a magical energy and a liturgical rite combined into a basic Mystery working. We will be using the element of Fire, because that is the element associated with the full moon. However, unlike the ritual associated with a traditional lunar esbat, we will be adding another component or variation of the energy worked, and that will be a vortex. I could write a book on the nature and quality of the vortex energy field, yet I believe that experiencing it for yourself would be the optimal teaching moment.[8]

---

8 Frater Barrabbas, *Elemental Powers for Witches*, 47–49. See these pages for a deeper definition of a vortex.

Liturgical Practices Performed in Sacred Space

A vortex is an energy field that is the opposite of the basic energy of the cone of power used for magical workings in Witchcraft. Where the cone of power is polarized along the periphery of the magic circle and fused in the center of the circle with a deosil spiral (as we shall see in Chapter Four), the vortex is where the watchtowers are drawn together to form a crossroads overlaid with a widdershins spiral from the outer circle to the center.

The circle charge is established by drawing an invoking pentagram of Fire at each of the watchtowers, yet the energy is fused together and projected through the floor of the temple into the point called the circle nadir. This combination of an energy field, drawing the crossroads, then performing a widdershins spiral walk from the outer circle to the center, and then projecting the power into the center of the circle and down to the nadir will generate an energy structure unlike anything you might experience in a traditional setting. However, this energy field, like a cosmic black hole, will resonate with the lunar energies, since it is the archetypal feminine energy.

A vortex is erected in the temple within the magic circle before the votive offering is made to the Deities and the lunar Mystery contemplated. In addition, there is the communion rite to be followed by the magical working (if there is any). Then the vortex is sealed since it cannot be banished. Later, the very same vortex could be unsealed and accessed if required. In this book, I will focus on sealing the vortex once the working is complete since layering multiple workings in a single vortex is a more advanced working than I wish to present here. The sealing spiral device is generated when the operator draws a spiral in the air with the wand, from the outside of the spiral circle to its center and in a widdershins direction. The sealing spiral is the opposite of an invoking spiral, which is from the outside to the center in a deosil direction.[9]

---

9   See Chapter Four for a definition of all four of the spirals that can be used with the wand.

A magical working is performed in its entirety within the lunar Mystery vortex and then it is exteriorized. We will cover how to develop and perform a basic energy working to manifest change into the mundane in Chapter Four, but for now, we will make a placeholder for that rite in the pattern of the Lunar Mystery vortex.

Here is the ritual pattern for the Lunar Mystery for a full moon esbat.

Lunar Mystery Full Moon Rite

1. Perform the circle consecration and any preparation steps required for a full temple operation.
2. Perform a brief meditation period to relax and adapt the proper mental state for the work.
3. Take up the dagger from the altar and proceed to the northern watchtower and draw an invoking pentagram of Fire.
4. Proceed to the western watchtower and do the same operation.
5. Proceed to the southern watchtower and do the same operation.
6. Proceed to the eastern watchtower and do the same operation. Fire pentagrams are now set to the four watchtowers.
7. Proceed to the northern watchtower and draw a line of force from the north to the center of the circle.
8. Proceed to the western watchtower and perform the same operation.
9. Proceed to the southern watchtower and perform the same operation.
10. Proceed to the eastern watchtower and perform the same operation. The crossroads are now drawn.
11. Proceed to the altar and set down the dagger and pick up the wand. Then proceed to the northern watchtower, bow, and then face the west and proceed to slowly walk with a purposeful stride around the magic circle,

proceeding widdershins. Slowly arc toward the center of the circle, passing the northern watchtower three times and then ending in the center. During this walk, use cool breathing to channel the energy, building up to a crescendo and then projecting the energy into the nadir in the center of the circle. The vortex is now set.
12. Perform the full votive working with offerings. The meditative session should be focused on the qualities of the full moon as associated with the full moon book that has already been developed.
13. Perform the communion rite for the special personal Deity, as discussed below.
14. Perform the magical working if there is one.
15. Stand up, bow before the shrine, and address each Deity, thanking them for attending your Mystery ritual.
16. Draw sealing spirals to the four watchtowers, starting in the north and proceeding deosil to east, south and west.

This ritual allows for flexibility with what is contained in the magical working and how it is to be performed. You should write up a version of this rite with all the steps and then practice it until you can perform it smoothly and without any awkward moments. I would recommend that this rite be performed for every full moon month, if possible, for a two-year period. Completing that task will ensure that you will have mastered this rite and know it fully.

Seasonal Sabbats

The seasonal sabbats are also religious and magical events, but they often have more of a community celebratory and feasting nature than an actual Mystery. However, if you want to perform a private Mystery ritual for a sabbat, then you can use a ritual pattern like the one used for the lunar esbat. For the eight sabbats, you would use an elemental energy related to the zodiacal sign for the sabbat, regardless of whether it is cardinal or fixed.

I have already noted the element associated with the sabbats in the table found in the previous chapter, page 43.

Instead of a negative vortex, for this sabbat Mystery, you would use a positively charged vortex using a deosil (sunwise) spiral instead of a widdershins spiral. The reason for using the positive vortex is that it emulates the archetypal masculine energies of the Sun, although the Sun can be depicted by a Deity that is gendered masculine or feminine. The temple can be decorated with traditional decorations associated with the sabbat and the officiant should write some prayers and a Mystery concept upon which to contemplate after the votive offerings.

Here is the ritual pattern for the sabbat rite.

Solar Mystery Sabbat Rite

1. Perform the circle consecration and any preparation steps required for a full temple operation.
2. Perform a brief meditation period to relax and adapt the proper mental state for the work.
3. Take up the dagger from the altar and proceed to the eastern watchtower and draw an invoking pentagram of the chosen element representing the sabbat.
4. Proceed to the southern watchtower and do the same operation.
5. Proceed to the western watchtower and do the same operation.
6. Proceed to the northern watchtower and do the same operation. Element pentagrams are now set to the four watchtowers.
7. Proceed to the eastern watchtower and draw a line of force from the east to the center of the circle.
8. Proceed to the southern watchtower and perform the same operation.
9. Proceed to the western watchtower and perform the same operation.

Liturgical Practices Performed in Sacred Space

10. Proceed to the northern watchtower and perform the same operation. The crossroads are now drawn.
11. Proceed to the altar and set down the dagger and pick up the wand. Then proceed to the eastern watchtower, bow, and then face the south and proceed to slowly walk with a purposeful stride around the magic circle, proceeding deosil. Slowly arc toward the center of the circle, passing the eastern watchtower three times and then ending in the center. During this walk, use cool breathing to channel the energy, building up to a crescendo and then projecting the energy into the nadir in the center of the circle. The solar vortex is now set.
12. Perform the full votive working with offerings. The meditative session should be focused on the qualities of the sabbat as associated with the traditional sabbat that has already been researched.
13. Perform the communion rite for the special personal Deity, as discussed below.
14. Stand up, bow before the shrine, and address each Deity, thanking them for attending your Mystery ritual.
15. Draw sealing spirals to the four watchtowers, starting in the east, and proceeding widdershins to the north, west and south.

As you can see, there is no special magical working for this rite, but one could be added, if that is desired. I believe that it is also a good idea to fully celebrate the traditional holiday with your community or friends, and to particularly have a feast and to offer a thanksgiving to the Gods. Your community sabbat celebration will most likely not be on the exact dates of the sabbat, but you will have already done your duty as a priestess or priest with your own private Mystery rite. Like the lunar rite, I would plan two annual cycles of sabbat Mystery rites to ensure that you have mastered the ritual.

INVOCATION OF DEITIES AND COMMUNION RITES

A core practice in the religious rites of a Witch is the combination of godhead invocation and communion. While offerings are given to the pantheon, only that Deity to which one has a special relationship and strategic alignment is the Goddess or God that is singularly invoked and summoned to be present for the giving of special offerings from the Gods. This calling and summoning is heartfelt, soulful, intimate, and empowering. This special Deity was called initially, as are all the Deities in the pantheon, and then the officiant performs a special calling to summon it, once the plate of sacramental offerings is laid upon the shrine.

As I have stated previously, mixing some foreign words from the culture of the pantheon into this invocation helps to amplify the energy associated with the invocation. These words can act as a kind of barbarous words of evocation that harkens back to the ancient times when this Deity was worshipped in that culture. Of course, English is appropriate for an English speaker, but adding foreign words to the invocation can act as words of power, whether or not they are understood. If you don't know what language to use, try Latin. There are several web-based translators to help you to translate your foreign words from English, and how to pronounce them.

This Goddess or God is called to appear and to come down and bless the food and drink with its essence, thereby infusing this fare with a bit of its being. Once that is done, while the officiant kneels with their head bowed in a pose of reverence, then the food may be consumed by the officiant or used for other purposes. However, this blessing of food and drink is always followed by the request of the officiant for the Deity to share this sacramental bounty, because such fare belongs to it and is given to the officiant as a sign of love and a token of benevolence. The officiant partakes of this food and drink with the knowledge that they are taking into their living body the essence of the godhead, thereby briefly making themself like unto the Gods.

Performing this rite on a monthly and seasonal schedule will introduce to the practicing Witch the power and utility of sacraments. Of all the systems or methods of magic, working with magical sacraments is one of the highest and most potent operations. Not only can the sacraments be consumed to permanently alter and transform the recipient, but they can also be used to charge objects and make them sacred artifacts. In addition to food and drink, the practicing Witch can also bless other substances, such as oils, unguents, salves, and other types of herbal drinks and remedies. They will use the same rite of communion to bless these other substances, allowing their favorite Deity to charge and transform them into sacramental substances.

Here is the ritual pattern for the Invocation and Communion rite.

Sacramental Communion Rite

1. Bow and kneel before the shrine and say the following words:

   "I seek from you, O beauteous God/Goddess, X, this boon and blessed favor from your hands and your heart."

2. Kneel in meditation until you sense some kind of affirmation from your chosen Deity.
3. Then rise and proceed to the altar and retrieve the dish of bread/cakes and the chalice of beer/wine and take them to the shrine, placing the dish and chalice separate from each other. (If there are other items to be blessed, they are placed with them.) Then, back away a few steps and kneel before the shrine.
4. With hands and arms held out in entreaty, and with your eyes upon the statue or place marker for the chosen

Deity, recite the invocation to the Goddess or God with passion and conviction, imploring the Deity to descend upon the shrine and bless the food and drink set aside for that purpose. You should say this invocation three times, and the last time it should be most emphatic. Then make the sign of the invoking pentagram over the dish and chalice.[10]

5. Bow with the head to the floor and crouch there for a short period of time while the Deity blesses the sacraments.
6. Then arise, still kneeling, and say the words:

"You have blessed my shrine with your powerful spirit and made my offering imbued with your essence. I seek a boon to partake of this sacramental food and drink so that you and I might be one."

7. Bow with the head to the floor and then arise to standing.
8. Proceed to the shrine and drink from the chalice and then eat one of the pieces of bread or cake. Leave the rest to be consumed by the Gods (or used later for sacramental refreshment or magical purposes).
9. Then back away a few steps, kneel and bow once more. Say the words:

"I have partaken of your essence, and now you and I are as one. May I always be worthy and properly prepared for your love. Thanks be for your hallowed blessings."

10. Bow a final time and then arise. The rite is ended.

---

[10] Use the invoking pentagrams of spirit creative or receptive, depending on the gender of your Deity or its outward character expression. See Chapter Four for how to draw the invoking pentagrams.

Liturgical Practices Performed in Sacred Space

The prepared invocation should be developed, written, and memorized, in addition to the other liturgical texts that you have developed for the Deities of the pantheon. This invocation is special because it is much more intimate and passionate. It represents the fact that you have chosen this specific Goddess or God to receive the greater share of your love and attention. Since you are also giving offerings to the other Deities in your pantheon, there is no possibility that you will create any offense by giving yourself to only one of them. The Deity that you focus on is the primary godhead in your family of Deities, and the rest are honored but are secondary to the one that you have chosen to bond with.

Pagans in antiquity saw the focus on one of many Gods as completely acceptable behavior, and they called it *henotheism*. The key concept is that you can focus on one Deity if you also honor and worship the others as well.

There is also a very important reason to focus and develop an intimate relationship with one of the Deities in a pantheon, and that is to prepare you for the more advanced stage of godhead assumption, developing the godhead as your spiritual embodiment, and godhead personification. These are advanced practices that require several years of work, devotion, and development. What I am proposing here is the first step in that direction. Godhead invocation and sacramental communion is an important part of the practice of a Witch.

Developing a Shrine of Deities and Ancestors

While the main altar is the place where tools are kept and items that are to be used temporarily are placed, the focal point for liturgical practices is the shrine. The shrine is where the Deities or their place markers reside. It is also a place where you can place a picture of a special ancestor or even a departed teacher. It is where votive offerings are made, prayers are directed, and the focus of meditations and trance work.

Mastering the Art of Witchcraft

Special tools or precious items are placed on the shrine as permanent gifts given to the Gods, items that can no longer be owned or claimed by mortal humans. There are votive candles, one of the watchtowers, an incense burner, plates, a flower vase to hold flower offerings, and cups and dishes to hold offerings. Sometimes the shrine table is larger than the main altar because it must hold so many things.

The shrine should also be kept clean and tidy, and offerings properly disposed of when no longer needed. The wall behind the shrine can also be where a picture or painting of the favored Deity is placed. If decorations are scant in the rest of the temple, the shrine is richly decorated. The cloth that covers the shrine table can be fancy, embroidered, and brightly colored. If the temple is temporary, then the shrine can be covered with bed sheets to obscure it from profane eyes when not in use, but the table should always be left in its place, unlike the rest of the furniture.

Place markers for the Deities in the Witch's pantheon can be miniature statues, small busts, precious coins with a Deity's face, or a beautiful rock or crystal. How it becomes a place marker is that it is officially placed on the shrine with a bit of pomp and drama when the circle is consecrated, and from that point on, it becomes a place marker by the power of association. This is done for each of the elected Deities in the Witch's pantheon. Then, other place markers can be added over time. However, the place marker for the special Deity that is one's primary focus should have a place marker that is special and more defined than the others. It is the very first place marker to be added to the shrine, and the event of that placement is both dramatic and significant.

Small votive candles should be lit whenever there is some kind of working, and seven-day or fourteen-day glass-enclosed votive candles can be left lit until they burn completely down. Still, I am always leery of any kind of flame in an enclosed room, so that is why I have been attracted to battery-operated votive candles that appear to flicker like a real candle. I have also used oil lamps placed on the shrine and the main altar to help illuminate the temple. Incense offerings are given daily, and offerings of alcohol are typically very welcome and can be given weekly before they disappear. Maintaining the shrine will take a great deal of daily effort, but the spiritual alignment and self-empowerment that it creates make such work highly rewarding.

Self-Dedication Rite

The first step in developing any kind of alignment or connection with a Deity, and in this case, it should be the primary Deity in your pantheon, to be witnessed by the other Goddesses and Gods in that family, is the dedication rite. This ritual should be first performed when you have everything developed and worked out and you are ready to begin your work in earnest. I cannot stress how important this step is, and it is one that you should take at some point in your work as an independent practicing Witch. Even if you belong to a coven or a group and you are already initiated or in the process of being initiated, this step is something that is quite independent and unique to your own spiritual and magical practice.

This rite is also something that is not done just once and then forgotten simply because it entails certain periodic obligations upon you to worship your Deities and to perform your magic in a condition of solitude. A dedication rite should also be periodic as everything else that the Witch does. These are obligations that are between you and your Deities, and they cannot be delegated, shared, or somehow ignored.

What I have found is that even I, an elderly and experienced Witch, must perform a dedication rite to renew my alignment and reestablish my connection to my Goddesses and Gods in an objective manner. Whenever you drop your discipline for various reasons and neglect your spiritual and magical responsibilities, then performing this simple dedication rite will be the first step that you will take to begin your spiritual and magical work anew.

Here is the simple dedication[11] that even I have recourse to using periodically.

---

11   Frater Barrabbas, *Transformative Initiation for Witches*, Part One, Chapter Four—taken fully and with permission.

Dedication Rite

This rite should be performed in a consecrated and empowered circle, but it can be performed in any place that is private, such as in a grove or a backyard. The dedicant should bring votive offerings to the Deities (one or more for each), and these can be food, drink, incense, oil, or a special gift (crystal or semi-precious stone). The best place to perform this rite is in front of a shrine with statues or markers for the Deities in plain sight. A dedication oath can be written before the rite occurs and then read at the proper moment. I am including an example of what might be used as a dedication oath. This dedication is performed to each of the Deities that are a part of your pantheon, with a special focus on the primary one that you are engaging in.

1. Bow before the focus point where the Deities are perceived to reside, then briefly kneel.
2. Light incense and candles, present the Deity with the offerings, and say:

    "O [Deity Name], I make an offering before you so that you may find it good and true. But I shall make a greater offering, and that is myself." Then bow down before the altar.

3. Say dedication:

    "I, [Witch Name], in the presence of [Deity Name] do swear to serve, love, and worship you, making these offerings to you, but offering my life and spirit to be in your hands for whatever destiny you deem is suitable. May I receive your knowledge of hidden things and may I stand in the light of your power. I make this vow and

dedicate myself to you and may my magic turn against me and the curse of the Gods be upon me if I break this most solemn and holy oath."

4. Offer the special gift, saying:

   "I give this precious offering to you, may it serve as a symbol of my love and faith."

5. If required, the dedicant can also make an offering of their own blood, using a sharp knife to make a small, shallow wound and to capture a drop or two onto a piece of cloth or parchment.[12] Then offer the blood to Deity with the rest of the offerings.
6. Stand up from the kneeling position, bow the head, and then extend the arms forward to the focus point, saying:

   "From my head to my feet, and all that is between them, belongs to you forever."

---

[12] During this procedure or any others herein, please use the utmost caution and care whenever skin is broken. Follow basic first aid practices of cleaning and dressing wounds, use sterile materials, and always dispose of blood and other bodily fluids responsibly. If bleeding ever becomes uncontrollable, promptly seek medical advice.

CHAPTER 4

PRACTICAL MAGICAL WORKINGS PART ONE

SINCE WE HAVE DISCUSSED what is the first half of the work of the solitary Witchcraft, which are the liturgical rites, we can now progress to the next half of the work, which is magic. The curious thing about Witchcraft is that it's a perfect blend of religion and magic. While establishing a powerful bond with the Deities of one's choice is a noble effort, the foundation this practice builds is the perfect platform to project magical powers and sacred blessings affecting the material world. The objective is the ultimate manifestation of the Gods. The method employed is a magic that bends probabilities and infuses the material and mundane world with the glamor of the Deities of nature. Therefore, a Witch does not do magic unaided or without the support of their elected Goddesses and Gods.

Magic is not the answer to all our problems and needs, and in fact, it is seldom able to make the impossible a possible realization. The material world has its limitations, and sometimes those limitations can narrow the field of possible constructive outcomes. It is a fact of life that we sometimes cannot change outcomes, but we can be more agile, insightful, prepared, and persevering to find the best available and optimal possibility.

Thus, magic is an important aid to a life lived in a material and secular world, but it is not the only work or means that a Witch employs to find their way through the maze of life. I believe that wisdom derived over time and through the resolution of life's trials is the final arbiter of a successful material life.

So, what exactly is magic and its function? That is the key question in considering the magical work of a Witch. Aleister Crowley defines magic as the art of causing change to occur in conformity with one's will. That seems to be overly simplistic and would therefore include many methods and techniques that would not be considered magical. It is obvious that magic employs some kind of ritual artifice and symbolic manipulation. While the will powered by desire and need is the driver of this work, the medium that the work employs is indirect and highly symbolized. Magic is a phenomenon of consciousness since it is highly subjective and individualized, but it also shares a common language, religious symbology, conscious artifacts, and cultural beliefs and expectations within the cultural collective. Magic that is employed in a country in West Africa would be quite different than that employed in Europe or the U.S., but there would be common characteristics despite the cultural differences.

I would define magic as the means to make changes in the material world or the self through the means of symbolic manipulation, within the conscious state where religious beliefs are grounded. My hypothesis stipulates that there is a close relationship between the linguistic world of symbols within the individual and collective minds of human beings and the material world and that a change in one promotes a change in the other. The symbolic world within consciousness is connected to attributes in the material world, and they interact with each other. Changes in the material world affect the conscious minds of individuals and cultures, but correspondingly, changes in the conscious domain can, through the artifice of symbols, affect the material world. This domain of consciousness, which is shared in our cultural collective, is where magic has a functional reality, magical powers exist, archetypal symbols have resonance, religious experiences are grounded, and spirits and Deities reside. We use meditation and trance to enter this world, and we learn by experience to perceive and interact with it.

Something that magic is very proficient at doing is helping to give a greater underlying meaning and significance to the unremarkable occurrences that happen to everyone. Many people pass through life reacting to whatever happens to them and retaining only the most dramatic occurrences in their memory. A magical operation for a specific need or desire makes that thing very important and strategic, associating more meaning and significance to it. Whatever happens will be remembered quite clearly over time, making that event important in one's memory.

Since magic is unable to perform miracles or make events that are highly improbable as possible, the question that you might have about it is, what *can* magic do? Magic is very good at bending probabilities, so anything that is a potential possibility can be made into an actual outcome. However, any magical rite that you might perform must also have mundane steps to help make it manifest. You can't just work magic and then expect your desired outcome to occur with little or no work.

Everything that you do must be earned, so working magic is accompanied by practical steps to ensure that all that can be done to make something a reality is covered. You might ask the question, "If magic requires accompanied mundane steps, then why bother to work it?" We work magic because *we can do it*, and this will add a certain weight to getting the outcome that we desire. We also work magic to make our desire more meaningful by associating it with powerful archetypal symbols within the magical sphere of consciousness. When we work magic, we also bring our alignment with our Deities into the equation, and this, too, will add more weight to the outcome. Following some basic practical rules about magic will make such work more successful.

1. Explore your current situation and the nature of what you desire by performing extensive divination using more than one methodology.
2. Never seek an outcome that is impossible.
3. If what you are seeking is within the realm of probability, then magic can be successfully employed if the other steps that you would normally need to perform are also done.
4. Take responsibility for the outcome of either achieving or failing to achieve your desire.
5. Make certain that there is nothing in yourself that might block the desired outcome. This can be verified by step one.
6. Limit your objective to just one thing. Complex objectives are much more difficult to achieve and are subject to failure. Make sure that your desired outcome is clearly defined.
7. Ensure that your objective is ethical and guilt-free.
8. Reducing the focus of your objective can assist in opening the door to other unanticipated possibilities. When seeking love, avoid casting a love spell on one person. Instead, make yourself a focus of lovability. When seeking a job or money, focus on the general outcome, a job, or money from some source, instead of focusing on one specific job or one specific source of money. There may be obstacles that are beyond your control.
9. When magic and mundane actions fail to deliver a desired outcome, then this is an important teaching moment. Find out why the operation failed. Use divination to help. Look over the rules above to determine if you violated any of them. Ask yourself, do you really want this objective? A failure is always an invitation to refine and perfect your magical work.

If you carefully follow the above nine rules of the practical application of magic, then you will experience far more successes than failures. Additionally, failures will teach you more about how your magic works than any successes you might have while learning to master this art.

It is my belief that these rules and practicalities associated with working magic will help you to achieve the outcome that you desire. They will help you understand what is needed to ensure that you have a successful ritual working. Now that we have defined what magic is and how it might be used, we should discuss the details about performing magical workings and making them a part of your liturgical practices.

This chapter will cover the basic knowledge and strategies that you will need to develop your own magical workings. You will need to know about timing, ethics, and practical magical considerations. We will examine the magic pentagram and how to use it to generate magical energies. We will also cover the basics of sigil magic and examine some basic ritual structures that you can use. Still, the last section will reveal the techniques for performing a divination session, probably one of the most important workings that you will perform. As I have said, divination functions as the eyes and ears of the Witch, so extending the boundaries for gaining information is quite important.

Timing, Ethics, and Magical Considerations

Before we dive into the specific techniques of working magic, we will need to briefly cover the topics of timing, ethics, and how to properly determine a magical objective. These are the *when*, the *why*, and the *what* associated with a magical objective. You will need to make these determinations very clearly defined before you move forward with writing and performing a ritual working to help achieve your goal.

The nine rules that I listed above could have been placed here, but I felt that those rules would help to define what magic is and how it is deployed before getting into the details about clearly defining an object. We will refer to and expand on those rules in this section, but they are an important part of defining what magic is and how it supposedly works or would fail to work if other factors are omitted or ignored.

WHEN TO WORK MAGIC: Since the kind of magic that I am discussing in this book is based on simple energy workings, then when to work this kind of magic is within the range of *not too soon* and *not too late*. You should work a magical operation close to when that magic will be needed to bend the probabilities. Performing this kind of magic too early or too late will likely diminish the probability of a desired outcome. You will also need to take mundane steps to help make this objective a more likely outcome. Coordinating the mundane steps with the magical operation when the Moon is waxing toward full will require some careful planning.

The event of the magical working should happen at some point between the new moon and the full moon. Since the full moon Mystery working that we have examined has a place in it for magical workings, that means that the full moon Mystery could be performed just before the actual full moon event if a specific magical working is planned. All the other steps and preparations will be expected to happen before this big magical event. You should make certain that the event of the magical ritual will occur just prior to when it is needed, so you will have to plan your calendar of mundane events accordingly to synchronize everything.

What this means is that if you are to schedule an important job interview, make that first important date with a potential loved one, or face any mundane deadline with the desire to empower it with a magical working, then you will need to schedule the working in the correct Moon phase. If you can't synchronize that deadline date with the proper phase of the Moon, then you can just perform a magical working without the Lunar Mystery rite so that the magic occurs before the deadline. The Moon must be waxing when the magic is performed, so that is the only restriction that might need to be considered.

Why to Work Magic: This approaches the ethical considerations for working magic on a specific objective. It is important to fully understand the motivations behind working magic since that will inform you if you are acting in an ethical manner. Coercion, dominance, and exploitation are to be avoided if possible. So is working any kind of malefic operation unless it's fully justified. Also, avoid any kind of magical working that might give you a guilty conscience if you are successful. To be ethically clear, you should not have any qualms or second thoughts about what you are about to do.

Additionally, if your rationale for working magic is something that would benefit more than just you, then you can consider yourself on solid ground. Like life itself, if your motives are negative, completely selfish, coercive, or exploitative of others, then performing magic to aid such an endeavor will incur ill-favor with not only the people around you, but the Gods themselves. Malefic magic can be worked against another if it is fully justified since there is no cost associated with defending yourself and your friends and family from external threats. Selfish motivations and the desire to inflict unjustified pain will likely bring you more trouble than any benefits.

What to Work Magic Upon: It is important to refine and clarify your objective so that it is easy to symbolize it and to determine success or failure. As I pointed out in the nine rules of magic, complex objectives make the process of symbolizing it and measuring its success difficult. It also can introduce confusion and internal conflict (crossing) into the mechanism to successfully achieve the desired outcome. Additionally, it is a wise approach to make your goal flexible, instead of narrowing it down to a single thing, like a specific job opportunity or a specific love interest. Apply magical energy to yourself for self-empowerment, since this often will give you the additional confidence needed to be successful. Ensure that achieving your goal is eminently justified, especially if it is to punish or battle other people. Whatever you decide to do with your magic, make certain that you take responsibility for your actions whether the magic succeeds or fails. Knowing what to do when the magic is successful is as important as the mitigating steps needed when the magic fails.

The magical techniques that I will be describing in this book are based on the energy model of magic. We will be using the more simplistic methods for generating, imprinting, and projecting magical energy to make something in the material world occur. There are many other more sophisticated techniques and systems of magic that can be learned, but this technique is the easiest to adopt. We will discuss this methodology more fully when we talk about the magic pentagram.

Tool Consecration Rite

The dagger and wand will need to be consecrated if they are to be made ready for magical workings. You can consider this to be your first magical objective. The basic idea is to bless and charge the tool with sacraments already available to you. That would be incense smoke, lustral water, and some kind of perfumed consecration oil. The oil doesn't need to be charged and blessed, and neither does incense. The lustral water should be readily available for use since it is generated during the circle consecration rite. You can also consider touching the tool with a fragment of consecrated bread to aid in its sacralizing.

This operation is performed during a full moon Mystery rite after the communion rite, so all the sacraments should be available for use. It is also the point in the rite reserved for

Practical Magical Workings Part One

magical workings, so it will help you to learn to master that kind of working within the liturgical rite. Here are the steps that you should follow.

1. Perform the Lunar Mystery full moon rite up to step fourteen. This is where magical workings will be performed.
2. Lay the tool to be consecrated on the altar upon the ceramic pentacle.
3. Sprinkle lustral water on it.
4. Smear a dab of perfumed oil on it.
5. Touch a fragment of consecrated bread to it.
6. Use the thurible to incense the tool thoroughly.
7. Place both hands on the tool, bow the head, and say the following:

"Oh Wand/Athame of Wisdom/Power, I charge and bless you in the name of X, that you may serve me in my magical endeavors."

8. Look up to the ceiling and imagine a ray of light descending from there down onto your hands and the tool beneath.
9. Step away from the altar and bow, then return to retrieve the tool. Immediately use it, either making invoking spirals or drawing lines of force with it.

I would recommend blessing and charging both tools, one after the other, in the same rite and making them fully prepared for future magical workings. You can use tools that are not consecrated to perform liturgical operations, since by using them as such, they will be magical tools. However, the dagger and the wand should be blessed and charged in a consecration rite so that they might emulate the archetypal nature of these two tools.

Magic Pentagram—Basic Energy Working

The magical pentagram is the heart of magical workings that use the energy model of magic. This is because the five points of the pentagram are associated with the four elements and spirit. While the history of the four elements and their use in magic is complex and has an ancient provenance, we can take it for granted that the four elements represent the archetypal energies to be used in our magical work. Let us examine the pentagram in greater detail and discuss the nature of the four elements.

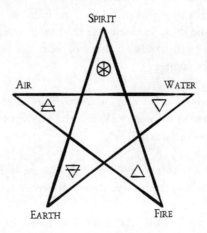

How the magical pentagram is deployed is that it is drawn in the air with the dagger. You always aim the dagger to the point opposite of the elected element and then draw the pentagram from that point, following the outline toward the elected element, then past it, following the lines of the pentagram outline until the final stroke is made from the opposite element to the elected element. Then you draw an invoking spiral over the pentagram, using a deosil arc, from the outer periphery to the center of the pentagram, projecting the energy from your body through the dagger into it. You use cool breathing to raise the energy and then exhale when the point is projecting power into the center of the pentagram. It is also a good idea to visualize the element when you are invoking it with a pentagram. I typically do this by imagining an energy that has a specific color.

There are two basic rules for drawing an invoking pentagram. The first is that you always point to the element opposite and draw toward the element that you have chosen to invoke. You will also avoid drawing the lateral lines running diagonally under the two arms of the pentagram when starting to draw the pentagram; that way, there will always be one point opposite the point that you have elected to invoke.

For instance, if you wanted to invoke the energy of Water, you would start at the point opposite, which is Air. And then draw toward the point that is Water, then continue to draw the pentagram until you come again to Air and then make the final line of power from Air to Water. There should be six lines drawn to form the pentagram, which is used to invoke a specific element. Drawing a pentagram device in the air in this manner will cause it to resonate and generate the chosen element at the place where it is drawn. To fill a magic circle with the chosen element, you will need to set that invoking pentagram to the four quarters.

To close or banish a pentagram that is emanating an elemental energy, you need to draw the opposite invoking pentagram and overlay it with a banishing spiral. In the case of closing the active pentagram of Water, you would draw the invoking pentagram of Air. To banish the invoking pentagrams for Fire and Earth, you would start at the elected element point and draw toward the point of Spirit, in effect performing an invoking of the pentagram of Spirit creative for Fire, or Spirit receptive for Earth. I know that this might seem strange, but what differentiates an invoking from a banishing pentagram is the spiral that is placed over it.

Here are the invoking and banishing pentagrams as they would be drawn to either generate or close a specific elemental device. You will note that there are also invoking and banishing pentagrams for Spirit as well. Since there is a right-hand and left-hand side to drawing the line from Earth or Fire to Spirit, these two invoking pentagrams will generate the attribute of Spirit, where the right-hand is for the creative (archetypal masculine) and the left-hand side is for the receptive (archetypal feminine) aspects of Spirit. Spirit is the quintessence or blending of the four elements into the fifth, which is the ether. It is the ether where all things are joined into the One.

These invoking and banishing pentagram devices differ somewhat from what you will find in the Golden Dawn or other Ceremonial Magical books that incorporate what is called the Superior Pentagram Ritual. The method that I am presenting here is based on what I was taught in the Alexandrian coven where I was first initiated into Witchcraft. I have found over the decades that the methodology I was taught is succinct and logical. There are always different ways to categorize and perform magical operations, and there is no authorized method unless you happen to belong to a tradition that has employed that kind of authority. When I examined the differences between how other traditions work their magic, I found that they are based on minor idiosyncrasies rather than sound, documented occult lore.

Additionally, I have omitted the lesser invoking and banishing pentagrams from my examples and methodologies because I have found that they are not needed in a Witchcraft magical context. Since we set, charge, and consecrate a magic circle before any kind of magical working, and then close it when the operation is completed, I have found that doing so performs the same operation as a lesser invoking and banishing pentagram rite. Therefore, these two pentagram devices, which employ the lateral lines of the arms of the pentagram structure, are not used. If you desire to employ this ritual, then you can seek how to perform it either from online sources or from any book on the Golden Dawn. We won't employ them in this work.

The spirals that are used with the magical tools, and in winding up and exteriorizing the energy in a magical circle, have basically two dimensions. These dimensions are the

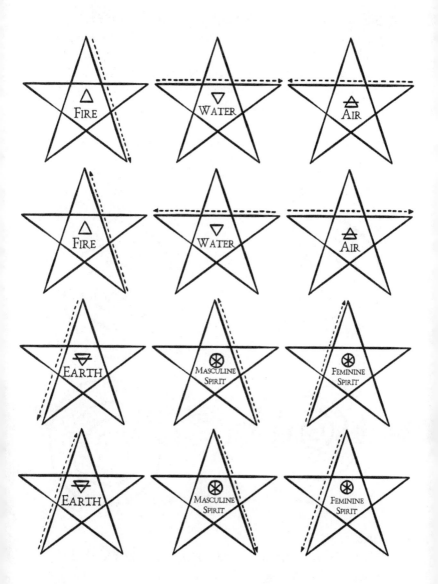

directions of deosil and widdershins, and from outside to inside and inside to outside. I have used directions wherever these spirals applied, but I wanted to place them here because they are a part of the energy work, like pentagrams. Applying these two dimensions together produces four spirals. We will use the invoking and banishing spirals and the sealing spiral but leave the unsealing spiral for more advanced workings. Here is a diagram showing the four different spirals that can be deployed using magical tools or walking within a magical circle.

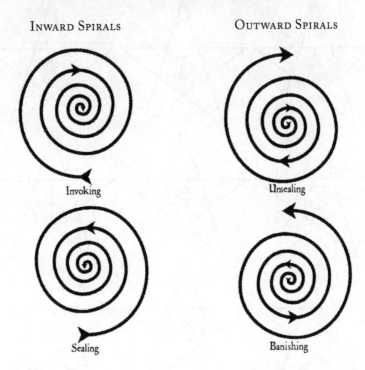

We have defined the means of invoking or banishing an elemental energy using a pentagram device. It is important that we define the qualities and nature of them to help in choosing one of them to empower a magical ritual. Each of the four elements has a specific metaphorical quality that distinguishes them.

Practical Magical Workings Part One

Fire: Action, inspiration, aspiration, creativity, beginnings, electric, expansive, archetypal masculine, ambition, aggression, fullness, light, a lightning bolt, realization, illumination.

Water: Passivity, reflection, reception, internalization, feelings, emotions, love, fear, magnetic, contractive, archetypal feminine, emptiness, darkness, intuition, visions, dreams, belief.

Air: Knowledge, mental activity, agility, expression, literacy, communication, agreements, opinions, conjecture, curiosity, intelligence, volatile, restlessness, bisexual, willpower, legality, theft, trade.

Earth: Life force, wealth, health, stability, pleasure, acquisition, material success, home, agriculture, fertility, spoilation, corruption, death, illness, infirmity, family, children, bureaucracy, money, regeneration, birth, healing.

Elements also have a polarity between them, as you will notice examining their qualities. Fire is polarized by Water, and Air is polarized by Earth. When all these four qualities are added together, we get the attribute of Spirit, which is more than the sum of their qualities. The quality of Spirit is union, the source, the ether that connects everything together into one thing, the domain in consciousness where magic exists along with the power of the four elements, spiritual beings, and Deities.

When working magic with the elements, you will use the invoking pentagram to generate a specific elemental energy by projecting this device to each of the four quarters and the center of the circle. Walking an invoking spiral in the magical circle will wind the energy up into the center of the circle, where it is projected into the invoking pentagram residing in the zenith. The energy is then ready to be imprinted with your desire or objective, symbolized as a character or seal that is part of the next magical technique we will explore. It is the use of the sigil developed by the operator that will be used to imprint the energy field, so when it is released, it will be exteriorized into the material world to affect the target of the operation. We will discuss more about that in the final section, but first, we need to discuss the art of making sigils.

Sigil Magic: Signs, Seals, and Witch Marks

Sigil magic is a discipline and methodology all by itself, and I would recommend that you investigate and master this magical technique as you also study and work with the material in this book. What we will cover is how to produce a single sigil device that you can use to imprint the magical energy that you have generated using the invoking pentagrams.[13]

You would start this technique by writing down in as few words as possible the objective that you wish to realize. Eliminate obvious words such as "I," "desire," or "will" from the phrase so that what you have is reduced to just the essential words.

For instance, the objective "I need a new job" would be reduced to "need new job" or even "new job." I will go with "need new job" to make a sensible phrase.

The next step is to take that phrase and eliminate any redundant letters. So, "need new job" would become "NEDWJOB," so that is the phrase that we want to turn into a sigil.

Then we need to eliminate letters that are variations of each other based on their shape. In the phrase "NEDWJOB," we can identify "N" and "W" as having the same vertical and diagonal lines. The curves for "D," "J," and "B" would be represented by a curve that faces to the left and one that faces the right, along with vertical and horizontal lines that are already represented in the previous elimination. What is left is the "O," which can be used to complete the structure. I typically make the "O" into a

---

13   Frater Barrabbas, *Elemental Powers for Witches*, 121–131. See these pages for a deeper discussion of constructing sigils for magical operations.

small circle added to the overall form. What we are left with are the basic forms of the letters, and it would look like this example.

BASIC
SHAPES

Then taking these basic forms, assemble them together to make a character where they are used as a single unit. You can experiment with how that might look, and this is where some creativity comes to play in this art. This would be the sigil representation of your objective, and you would draw it on a piece of parchment that would be blessed in the communion rite. Then, when you generate the elected element charge, you would use the sigil parchment to project that image into the energy field before exteriorizing it.

FINAL
SIGIL

Consecrating the parchment sigil is where it is transformed into a seal that will act as a symbol for your magical working. You can keep the parchment sigil or seal after the magical working is completed, and then burn it once the Moon passes the full moon mark.

This is the simplified method for creating a sigil. If you want to write something using a magical alphabet to embellish the sigil, then you can use the Theban alphabet to disguise your writing. You can also use it to write the names of your Deities on placards and place them in front of your Deity place markers.

You can find an example of the Theban alphabet in many places on the internet. I refer to the Theban alphabet as the "Witch Marks" since it is often associated with magical writing in the art of Witchcraft.[14]

Basic Ritual Spell Structures

We have a single but very useful ritual pattern, or spell structure, to employ the energy model of magic in a very simplistic and direct manner. You shouldn't be fooled by the simplicity of the design of this ritual since it is quite effective and based on decades of experience. Because this rite is performed by a single operator, it will require a greater reliance on the imagination and bodily exertion than a similar ritual performed by a coven or group. If this ritual is performed as part of a full moon Mystery rite, then it will have the added power of the Gods in attendance than if it were performed without that Mystery rite.

To reach the stage of developing a pentagram ritual to power a spell, it must pass the assessments (the when, the why, and the what) described in the previous sections of this chapter. The product of that assessment and development is a clear objective, a consecrated sigil, a time for the work, and a thorough understanding of what needs to be done to achieve successful results. All the preliminary steps needed to develop and perform an elemental energy working have been covered previously. We are now ready to show the basic pattern for the Elemental Pentagram Energy ritual, which is what we are calling this ritual. It is a slightly modified cone of power that can be used by a single operator, and it has the same level of energy raising and projection as what a coven could produce with a less sophisticated cone of power. The key difference is using the invoking pentagram to generate the element energy field.

This ritual has five points where the invoking pentagram is set, and that is the four quarters and the center of the circle at

---

14 Johannes Trithemius, *Polygraphia*, c.1499.

the zenith. An invoking spiral (deosil outer to inner) walked upon the magic circle from the periphery to the center will compress the energy field so that it becomes a cone with a narrow beam of power centered within it. The operator will use the consecrated sigil to project the symbolized object into the energy field, and then they will walk a banishing spiral from the center of the circle to the outer periphery and project it outside of the circle and into the material world. The banishing spiral will exteriorize the energy and transmit it as a bolt of magical force, programmed with the symbolic essence of the desired objective. The operator will use breathing techniques to compress the energy and then project it out of the circle.

This ritual, if it is used in the full moon Mystery rite, will be performed at step fourteen; otherwise, it will be performed after the circle is consecrated.

Elemental Pentagram Energy Ritual

1. Perform this rite as step fourteen in the full moon Mystery rite or once the circle is consecrated. The operator is prepared for this ritual working, both mentally and physically.
2. The operator proceeds to the altar and takes up the dagger and then walks to the eastern watchtower. They then draw an invoking pentagram of the chosen element and then visualize the element energy. They say:

    "I summon the Element power of X in the name of the God/dess Y."

3. The operator proceeds to the southern watchtower and performs the same ritual action as previously.
4. The operator proceeds to the western watchtower and performs the same ritual action as previously.
5. The operator proceeds to the northern watchtower and performs the same ritual action as previously.

6. The operator proceeds to the center of the circle and performs the same ritual action as previously, except projecting it to the zenith. The fivefold energy field is now set.
7. The operator proceeds to the altar and sets the dagger down and picks up the wand (right hand) and the parchment sigil (left hand). They say:

"I shall bring this power to the center where it may be blessed and constrained."

8. The operator proceeds to the eastern watchtower, faces the south, and walks slowly and deliberately around the circle, moving deosil and arcing inwardly so that they pass the eastern watchtower three times, and then arrive in the center of the circle. While they are walking, they use cool breathing to gather the energy, and with the wand, project it before them. As they proceed, the passage becomes more difficult and the energy more resistant, yet they persevere.
9. Once in the center of the circle, they take the parchment sigil and hold it above their head, and look up, projecting the image of the sigil into the compressed energy field. They say:

"I use my will to make my desire realized! May the Gods make it so!"

Then they stand there for a moment, breathing in the compressed energy in the center.

10. The operator faces the east, then turns to the north, and proceeds to walk from the center slowly around the circle widdershins arcing to the outer periphery of the circle, using the wand to project the power before them. As they progress, they use the bellows breath briefly at intervals to super-charge the energy as they

push it forward. When they have passed the eastern watchtower three times, they continue their circular path until they arrive at the northern watchtower, where they lunge forward, pointing their wand, projecting the energy out of the circle into the material world.

11. After standing for a short period, they will proceed to the altar and leave the wand and the parchment sigil there. They will bow briefly and say:

"May the power do its work! The ritual is completed."

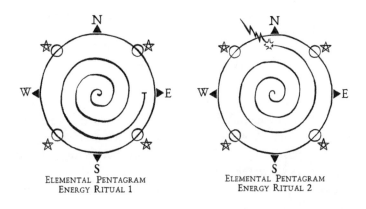

ELEMENTAL PENTAGRAM ENERGY RITUAL 1

ELEMENTAL PENTAGRAM ENERGY RITUAL 2

I have used more advanced variations of this ritual in the past four decades, and whatever the variation, it has always helped me to achieve my goals when I have applied the practical rules of magic to my objective. The Energy Model of magic is a very powerful and efficient method for working magic on material objectives. Like any energy, it must be used directly on the target and deployed when it is needed. Timing is important for this kind of magic.

Energy magic using just the four elements has its limitations, simply because the energies are too general. When these energies are combined to produce an element base combined with an element qualifier, then the elemental energy that is produced is more likely to match your objective. Such an evolution in magical energies would require a more advanced ritual pattern, so you should use this pattern until you have mastered it and are ready to work with more advanced energies and ritual patterns.

Now that we have covered this ritual pattern, I can note that we have introduced three ritual patterns for working with energy. We saw the negative vortex, the positive vortex, and the imprinted pentagram cone of power. These are the three ritual patterns using energy magic that you should study and experiment with so that they will become known energy structures to keep available in your magical toolbox. A creative Witch will find ways to use these ritual structures in other applications.

What we need to cover next in this chapter, and it is probably a very important ritual, is the divination session.

Divination Session

I have discussed previously that you should learn to master more than one method of divination, and that having a pair of dice or knucklebones to ask yes or no questions is the first and foremost kind of divination to be used. Selecting the odd numbers as a negative, and even numbers as a positive, you can throw the two dice and determine if the answer is affirmative or negative.

Who you will be asking these binary questions of are the Gods of your pantheon, either to one or to all. I would recommend that when you are about to start to develop a magical objective that you should ask the Gods if this is something that they sanction or approve. If the answer is affirmative, then proceed with your work; if it is negative, then you might think about it and delve deeper into it. Always address such a question to a specific Deity or name them in order of precedence.

Still, for important questions or in-depth research before a magical working is determined, then a divination session is the optimal way to proceed. That means you will perform your divination using the tools that you know how to use and do it in the sacred space of a consecrated circle. If it is a critical question or if there are dire circumstances that need to be investigated, then the divination session should be performed during a full moon Mystery rite. Otherwise, if you are just doing readings, or even doing readings for someone who is not privy to your private practice, then you needn't worry about doing it in sacred space.

Keep in mind that divination is a ritual performed where the Gods are asked to respond and aid you in determining the answer. Some questions cannot be answered, or some questions are so convoluted that they will need time, meditation, and mental insight to help break apart a complex request so that it can be examined. Like working magic, clarity and simplicity work best when performing a divination session.

Apart from the actual reading, you should also meditate and engage in prayer to the Deities of your pantheon. This will prepare the atmosphere of the magic circle for the Gods to reveal their Mysteries and secrets to you. Once the reading is completed, you should write down what was revealed, the time and date, and examine it at another time. You will also need to thank the Gods for their help and direction and make a simple offering to them of candles and incense.

Here is the ritual pattern that you can use when performing a divination session.

DIVINATION SESSION RITE

1. Consecrate the magic circle in the typical manner.
2. Perform an initial meditation session for fifteen minutes.
3. Perform a weekly votive offering to the Deities—skip step seven.[15]
4. Ring a bell or a gong three times (you can also clap three times).

---

15 This refers to step seven of the votive offering rite. See Chapter Three, page 54.

5. Then, looking at the shrine, say the following invocation:

"I seek a boon from you, my Gods, and from you, O my beloved X, that you open the doorways to understanding and insight so that I may receive your guidance through the divination that I now perform."

6. Perform the divination while sitting before the shrine. (I would recommend using at least two different methods).
7. Carefully examine the results of the reading, then write it down in your diary, noting the question asked, the date, the time, and the reading interpretation.
8. Bow the head and say the following:

"O my beloved God/dess X, I thank you for your guidance. Let me sleep upon this oracle and dream of anything that you would wish to impart to me regarding this issue."

9. Stand up, bow before the shrine, and address each Deity, thanking them for attending your prayer session.

10. Break the magic circle and give the Gods license to depart. The ritual has ended.

Make certain that you note any dreams that you might have during the evening. It is also possible that a dream might occur even a few days later. Be vigilant in case the answer doesn't come during the first night.

You should also revisit the reading a day or three after the session. Lay out the cards or rune stones in the pattern that they assumed during the reading and look at them with fresh eyes. It is possible that when revisiting the reading, new information may be revealed.

Practical Magical Workings Part One

What I have found when performing a divination session is that I usually try too hard to interpret the meaning of the reading. Later, when I have had time to analyze the results, I feel like a fool who asked an obvious question to the Gods. Sometimes hindsight will show that the answer was powerful and clear. Still, sometimes the Gods are fickle, or they want you to work for the answer, making the reading a teaching moment. Yet, if your answer was not clear or if it was hidden in subtle and symbolic meaning, then you might need to get a second opinion. This is where having a good peer group can help you when you encounter a Mystery or something that escapes your ability to understand. I have also found that an unclear response in the reading is made clearer in my dreams, but they occur days afterward.

Always remember that the responsibility for divination is yours alone. If you are not clear and precise in your questions, or if your questions are foolish, or if asking them is disrespectful to the Gods, then you might get some confusing, condescending, or even negative results. Be respectful and reverent and the Gods will help you overcome your inability to understand.

CHAPTER 5

PRACTICAL MAGICAL WORKINGS PART TWO

WE TURN TO ANOTHER BODY OF LORE that I believe is important for a solitary Witch to know, and this lore is more ancient and traditional to Witchcraft magic. However, due to the various religious currents affecting the Craft today, it is unlikely that the traditional methods of magical defense and offense are a part of the training regimen of groups or solitary practitioners. These spells and rituals employ archaic tools, such as cords, ancient words of power and poetic cantrips, the poppet or voodoo doll, the use of rocks, and enchanted rural locations. These archaic practices are as important as what I presented in the first part of practical magical workings, and they represent the expertise needed to advance to a more sophisticated magical practice. I also feel that it is necessary to remind you that your personal Deities are your greatest allies and that there are ways to incorporate them into your magic—if they are willing to aid you.

I learned this lore very early in my career as a Witch. Some of it was given to me by my teachers and some of it I picked up from various associates or cheap pulp books that I could afford in those times. However, much to my surprise, these methods had more fundamental principles behind them, which ultimately led to more advanced techniques and ritual lore. What was worked by me in those early years was carried forward because of the basic rules of magic that operated behind them. There are two specific rules or laws that make this kind of magic, and every other kind of magic, effective. These rules are the basis of sympathetic magic, which as parts of the psychological model of magic, are not primitive superstitions but potent mental algorithms. Allow me to explain them.

RULE OF CONTAGION: This rule states that objects that have once been in contact continue to act as if they were still in contact. Such a thing that binds or associates two things together is called a *link*. An item of clothing, nail parings, a cutting of hair, or a clot of blood are used to link that object with its owner. Since we now know that such items have traces of the owner's DNA, then such a consideration is hardly absurd.[16] However, this linkage is in the mind of the practitioner, and the work that is done with it is wholly within the mind. A link based on material objects or bodily substances is called a *physical* or *gross link*. It is, without a doubt, the most effective kind of link, but also limited to an extent.

RULE OF SIMILARITY: This rule states that like produces like, that an effect resembles its cause. Something that looks like the target or resembles it in some way can be a mental mediator for influencing or controlling that target. This is where the art of imitation has its power, producing effigies, fetishes, or poppets to affect the individuals that they are linked to, even when distant. A simplified form of this kind of work is the creation of symbols into seals or characters that linguistically embody a desire or objective. I have introduced that method to you as the fashioning of a sigil. *Similarity* also means

---

16   This also reminds me of Quantum Theory, especially particle entanglement.

translating something into its symbolic equivalent, and it will act as if it were the thing itself.

Similarity can also be represented as any system of correspondence, which is used extensively in forms of complex magic, such as elemental or planetary magic. The idea is that where symbolic qualities match up in a comparative table with certain baseline qualities, such as the four elements, the seven planets of the ancients, or any other quality, then those matching attributes are equivalent. Applying one automatically includes all the others that line up in a table of correspondences.

How these magical techniques work is based on the psychological model of magic. This model of magic is unlike the energy model of magic in that it assumes all magical phenomena are a product of the mind instead of a quality of energy. It includes the conscious mind of the individual, but also the greater mind of the collective. Language and linguistics are important parts of this kind of magic, since words symbolically characterize physical things, representing a powerful link between words (mental concepts) and material reality. Also, that magic has an element of "as if" built into it that allows for the transformation and translation of thoughts into form, and form into thoughts. It is the imaginative way children play, and it is the powerful system of metaphors that are an integral part of religious rituals, the arts, science, and magic.

Since consciousness is a phenomenon that we all are immersed and engaged in while we are awake, then there are two dimensions overlapping simultaneously. There is the individual conscious mind and there is the cultural collective mind in which individuals reside. The link between them is language, customs, beliefs, sentiments, protocols, and a whole host of other elements and attributes. It is a richly textured world and one where the individual and the collective constantly overlap. Additionally, in the highest states of consciousness, the greatest mystic sages have found that there is a point in individual consciousness where the individual melts away to be replaced by a state of union or oneness. That union is the unity of being, the final place of our ultimate spiritual return, and the likely place where consciousness had its origin.

As you can see, the psychological model of magic demonstrates that the rules of contagion and similarity are factual components of the universe of consciousness. If all things are connected into a oneness, then any act on an individual thing affects all things in some manner. It is within this concept of unified consciousness that things that were once connected are always connected, and things that are similar are, in fact, the same. These two rules operate in the psychological model of magic, showing that the artifacts of primitive magicians or shamans were and are potent tools in the hands and the mind of the wielder. It is the power of the trained and experienced mind against someone who has no clue what is affecting them or how. Thus, we should be cautious when exercising these kinds of magical tools.

We can proceed now to examine these other tools, knowing that they are potent and realistic artifacts to be included in any Witch's regimen of rituals and spells.

Binding and Releasing: Symbolic Cord Magic

Cords, used by Witches to work magic, are to be found in two different guises. The first is the working cord, such as the cord belt or cingulum that a Witch wears around their waist, and the second is the scourge, made up of seven to thirteen cords. There is also the cord that is used to take a Witch's measure when they are initiated into a coven and the three separate cords given to them as a gift at the conclusion of their initiation rite. Cords are used to bind a Witch during an initiation or for a hazardous rite, but these three cords used in that binding are those that are gifted to the initiated Witch by the coven, and one of them is used as a cingulum.

The scourge is a tool that is used in a coven setting and has no place in an independent practice, in my opinion.

Self-flagellation is an odd practice for a private need, and some might find it useful. Still, in my opinion, the scourge and the kiss are the tools of a very traditional coven, since the member in a submissive role would be bound and then scourged, to be released and followed with a kiss. These actions require at least two people, and in a working for just one, it becomes technically unfeasible. So, I have found that the scourge is a tool that I omit from my work unless required for a coven-style traditional initiation. The same is true with the measure, which I would never keep as a tool for controlling or coercing the members of a group, threatening them to obey me.

That leaves the working cords used to cincture the waist or to work cord magic. The key to simple cord magic is the artifice of the slip knot, which when the cord is pulled tight, the knot will be released. This fact represents the two actions associated with cord magic, and that is to constrict or constrain the flow of energy along the cord with a knot and then to release the energy built up in it. It is the power vested in Witchcraft, modeled on the magical use of the cord, to constrain spirits, bind individuals and things, compress energies, fix or immobilize minds and entities, and release them when desired or required. All these different abilities are associated with the art of cord magic, representing the ability to dominate and control the powers of nature, spirits, and even people.

We are not going to expound on cord magic in this book, but we do need to take the concepts implied by those techniques and apply them to more complex workings. The whole idea of using the art of ligature, bondage, and discipline as they are applied to magical workings is the basis of what we need to discuss and fully understand. Bondage and discipline represent a significant part of the use of cords in Witchcraft, and adding the scourge produces a complete package of BDSM, which was the apparent predilection of Gerald Gardner, the father of Gardnerian Witchcraft. Forgoing the scourge leaves us with the important actions of constraining, dominating (controlling), binding, and releasing, and it is these ritual actions that we will examine.

CONSTRAINING AND CONTROL: Constraining is the application of willpower, backed up by authority, to gain mastery over a situation, object, spirit, or person. It denotes the control and compression of objects, such as magical power that has been generated. Constraining magical power compresses and makes it more volatile and effective, like compressing a gas or steam vapor. We have already shown that feature when describing the steps in the Elemental Pentagram Energy Ritual example. When applied to a spirit, it represents the struggle to establish control and dominance, and this is where the individual's willpower, backed up by the authority of the Gods, becomes an important factor to determine who or what achieves the element of control.

Since the solitary practitioner is the priestess or priest of their own personal religious cult, their alignment to their pantheon of Deities, and most specifically to their primary Deity, does add to their personal empowerment and spiritual authority. When using their willpower to constrain an object, spirit, or person, that religious authority will make a considerable difference in a magical context. Their continual liturgical practices will give a greater feeling of confidence and personal empowerment when confronting troublesome spirits or people.

BINDING, LIMITING, AND IMMOBILIZING: Once constrained, an object, spirit, or person may be bound, which puts that entity or thing under the control of the Witch to either limit its ability to deviate from an ordained path or to fully immobilize it. This is where the operation of the constraint leads to complete domination and control. It is the symbolic expression of the use of the cords and the art of ligature to bind, control, and immobilize another. A symbolic binding with a spirit is to get its full cooperation, to reveal its secret name and seal, and to agree to a pact or quid pro quo arrangement. A symbolic binding upon a person is the infamous and traditional binding rite placed as a curse and as a dominating control mechanism on another. Ritual binding is a symbolic artifice that uses the power of binding combined with a simulacrum of the person being bound. It is a very common ritual talked about and discussed at length on the internet.

RELEASE, LICENSE TO DEPART, THANKSGIVING: When constraint and binding has achieved its goal, then it can be followed by a form of release. Like when a person or thing is bound with cords, those binding cords can be untied, and the subject is released from the bondage. A spirit that is constrained and bound is released through the artifice of a license to depart, which is a conditional release so that the spirit may fulfill its part of the pact or agreement. A Deity that is summoned and invoked is given a release through the grace of thankful farewell. A binding release on an individual is also a conditional release since it represents the fact that they have unwittingly obliged the operator who performed the binding.

We should complete this section with a ritual that you can use to bind a person, thing, or situation when and if it is required. This is a malefic rite that could damage the victim, particularly if they struggle against the binding, although this is a rare occurrence. To perform this rite, you will need to be fully and completely justified and have no doubt as to the rightness of the magical working. You should also perform this rite on someone with whom you have a personal acquaintance, even possessing some object or some blood, hair, or nail parings to help in building the link to the target. This is not a ritual that can be worked on someone who you only have a remote acquaintance with, such as a politician or celebrity. Like any kind of fight or act of retribution, it must be done to someone close and even intimate, and it requires passionate anger and even momentary hatred. This is not a ritual that works for the operator when their feelings are cold or indifferent.

Practical Magical Workings Part Two

Ritual of Binding

When all the means at your disposal to resolve the issue with someone have been met with failure or even spite, then it is time to get very angry and take your cause to the next level of magical work. What you will need to perform this ritual is a plain, misshapen rock, dark altar cloths, and a black robe. You will need to place black candles on the altar and shrine, and the watchtower lights filtered so that they cast a dim red light. A small amount of wormwood should be prepared in a ceramic cup, mixed with some potable liquor representing the poison to be dispensed to the victim.[17] You will need a black box with a lid, preferably one shaped like a coffin. The rock should be painted with the name of the victim written backward with a blood-red color, and it should be bound and wrapped with a black cord and secured in the box with another black cord. Thus prepared, you may begin this rite.

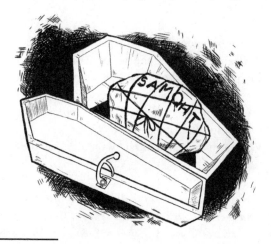

---

17   Always use caution when consuming herbal supplements of any kind, especially those known to have psychotropic effects. Do not consume wormwood in excess and seek medical attention if you experience nausea, vomiting, seizures, or any other unusual side effect. Persons with certain medical conditions should contact a medical professional before consuming wormwood.

Mastering the Art of Witchcraft

1. The circle is consecrated, black candles are lit, and watchtowers are illuminated, casting a blood-red light. If possible, you should apply dust and cobwebs to your person, making the black robe seemingly dusty with disuse.
2. Proceed to the shrine and perform a votive offering to the Deities. Call your personal Deity and silently request aid and the empowerment to perform this rite.
3. Standing before the shrine, focus on the victim, saying their name, and then saying it backward, again and again for a short period of time.
4. Say these words:

   "I summon my Goddess/God to aid me in this time of conflict and troubles. Help me to bind this person (name, then name backward) so that I might impose my will and greatly aid my cause."

5. Then bow before the shrine until you feel the energy shift and favor you and your mission. Only then may you proceed to the main altar to do your work.
6. The coffin with the stone imprisoned within is set upon the altar between the two black candles, and next to it is the cup of poison.
7. With arms spread and raised on high, say the following curse.

   "You (backward name) shall be turned into a stone,
   And that all your wits shall be turned front to back,
   And that over your face the loathsomeness will creep,
   And that as in a coffin, your limbs shall be bound,
   And that light shall be withheld from your eyes,
   And that your house and lands will be spoiled and impoverished,
   And that you shall be held as evil among your friends and family,
   And that all nourishment will taste like wormwood,

And that these things be so until I release you.
I spread this table and mark this stone.
And spit upon it [spit on stone] and conceal it.
And fix this curse upon you.
In the name of the foul fires,
Whose names are Ril, Yut, Sar, and Lod.
Who shall consume you as they are consumed."[18]

8. Light noxious incense in the thurible and incense the main altar with the coffin. Then asperge it with the symbolic poison in the cup. Then drink some of it, relishing in the bitterness.
9. Take up the dagger, then with hands and dagger raised above the coffin, descend the dagger until it touches the rock. All the emotions, anger, and passion are focused and directed on this rock sitting in a coffin.
10. Say these words:

"I have placed a powerful curse and a binding upon you, oh enemy of mine named (backward name). May it torment you until I deem to release you. You are under my power, and my will is the will of the God/dess [God/dess Name] that you shall be stopped in your tracks. I thus curse you!"

11. Rite is ended. Thoroughly clean the temple afterward and burn sweet-smelling incense.
12. Take the coffin and seal it up with another black cord. Then bury it on the victim's property or some place or path that they frequently occupy. Pour the rest of the contents of the poison cup over the spot.

---

18 Worth, Valerie. *Crone's Book of Magical Words*. Llewellyn Publications, 2002. 81–82.

Once the work has ended, use divination to learn and follow the results. Also, you must let the victim know, in some subtle manner, that you have cursed and bound them. That is the most important mundane step that you could take to help this magical work succeed. The mind is a terrible cauldron of fear and superstition, even for the most pious adherent or steadfast atheist.

Art of Incantation: Words of Power

If you have a gift for writing poetry, then you might be able to use that gift to write invocations, spells, and cantrips using the power and sound of words. If you lack this ability, then you can borrow and adapt poems or magical-sounding incantations from various sources. The nature of spellcraft, using words and sentences, rhythm and rhymes, powerful words and exhortations, or even words and phrases in another language, is a magical discipline that is completely self-contained.

Powerful words can replace symbolic actions or tool usages, at least to some extent. The ancient Egyptians believed that this was true, and their magic used a language crafted for their liturgies or magic that lector priests constructed and used. In the previous age in Europe, being literate was a magical power ascribed by the masses who were illiterate. Latin was the common language of academia, science, and magic.

Words of power are words that passionately describe facts, and they are often exclamations and potent orders or directives. You don't direct spirits, bless, or curse individuals, and project powers by using understatements and weak or overly elaborate phrases or sentences. Kings and emperors did not command by begging or using weak and feeble declaratives. So should you, as a powerful Witch, use words that have a powerful sound, commanding, passionate, and clearly stating desires and needs. Constructing these kinds of declaratives will require some wordsmithing, for certain. Although, I have often found that words of power can come unbidden or without deliberation when the emotions are engaged with speech.

Here is an example of how the Greco-Egyptians would have written a powerful evocation, using unknown words that have a powerful sound.

> "IAŌ IAŌ IAŌ I call upon you, Ptha Ra Ptha Iē Phtha Oun Emēcha Erōchth Barōch Thorchtha Thōm Chaieouch Archandabar Ōeaeō Ynēōch Ēra Ōn Ēlōph Bom Phtha Athabrasia Abriasōth Barbarbelōcha Barbaiaōch; let there be depth, breadth, length, brightness, Ablanathanalba Abrasiaoua Akramma Chamarei Thōth Hōr Athōōpō. Come in, lord, and reveal!"
>
> —*PGM XII*, lines 153–160[19]

Even though this evocation contains mostly unknown and difficult to pronounce barbarous words of power, also called *verba ignota*, it still has a powerful effect on the reader and the spiritual audience. It is very likely that the individuals who might have used this evocation or others like it would not have known what the words meant but would have used it regardless. It is the emphatic sounds expressing mysterious powers and antique sources that stir the mind and heart of the operator and reverberate throughout the temple.

You can use an antique language or one that you are unfamiliar with, or just use your native language, but make it sound powerful. I have found that the Enochian language is quite potent, even when used outdoors in a grove.

Here is another one for you to examine.

> "Emperor Lucifer, master of all the rebel spirits, I ask you to be favorable in my summons of your greater minister

---

19 See Betz, Dieter, *Greek Magical Papyri In Translation* 159.

Lucifuge since I wish to make a pact with him. I also request that you, Prince Belzebuth, protect me in my undertaking. O Count Astaroth be propitious and ensure that the great Lucifuge appears to me tonight in human guise and without emitting foul odors and that he grant me as per the pact I will present to him, all of the riches which I require."

— *The Grand Grimoire,* 26–27[20]

While this evocation might seem a bit tepid in its pronouncements, making demands on infernal spirits has its own degree of daring and empowerment. This evocation assumes that the devils summoned will be all too willing to grant their powers and authority to the operator, wherein the operator might enrich themselves at the mere cost of their soul. The devils obey the operator because of the spiritual purity and sanctity that this person holds, although what the operator does with that infernal power likely will undo their own special relationship with the Christian God. Of course, this kind of exchange would be ludicrous to a Witch, since they have no problem making quid pro quo deals with spirits, and that would not in any way abrogate their alignment and obligations to their Deities. The Christian God is, unfortunately, a jealous and unforgiving one.

Writing evocations, exhortations, hymns of praise, curses, and words to raise great and forbidden powers is the stuff of comic books and graphic novels, and the subject of your own ambitions if you seek to write your own rituals. I could give you endless examples of this art form, but in the end, it is up to you to be the author of your own incantations, evocations, and words of power.

---

[20] See Rudy, Gretchen and Venitiana del Rabina, Antonio, *The Grand Grimoire,* 26–27.

Poppet Creation and Magical Uses

Taking the rule of similarity and contagion to their conclusion reveals the most potent ritual in the arsenal of the Witch. This is the rite where the operator gives life and breath to a simulacrum designed as a human poppet.[21] Actions magically projected onto this poppet can bless and heal the associated target, or they can harm or even kill. The poppet is, of course, the infamous voodoo doll, and as a method of magic, it truly works. It incorporates the psychological model of magic, so the benefactor or victim will need to know, in some manner, that they are a target of this sorcery.

This magical work is called the *Grand Bewitchment*, and aside from the evocation of spirits through the agency of a familiar spirit, it is considered the apex of the magic of a Witch. However, it was one of the rituals that I came upon early in my career as a Witch,[22] and I have since come across several variations. The variation that I will present here was based on a ritual given to me by members of my coven since it was a popular ritual amongst the Alexandrian Witch community.

I have used this spell several times, but only to offer healings and blessings to help individuals and even myself. I was able to adapt this ritual from its original form since it required the assistance of a priestess to act as both the womb and midwife in the operation. I have never used this ritual to harm or kill someone, but I know from my own personal experience that it is a powerful spell for healing, so it would also be effective for harming someone. I will leave the ethical considerations for such a working to you.

If you are going to help someone with this rite, then you will need to be certain to engage them in this working so they

---

21 The poppet is also called a *fith-fath* in some traditions.
22 I found a version in Paul Huson's book *Mastering Witchcraft* early in my studies (192–199), but I was given another version when I joined a coven years later.

can fully absorb its effects. If you are working malefic magic using a poppet, then you will need to use subtlety and deceit to let them know that you are seeking to harm them. Letting someone know, however subtly, helps to close the circuit in establishing a link in this spell, and additionally, once this rite is completed, if it is used to harm someone, the operator would need to disconnect and disassociate themself from this working so that it would not rebound.

Ritual of Grand Bewitchment

The first stage of this spell is to construct a poppet. You can use wax, clay, paper mâché, or cloth. You can dress it up in simple clothes and affix a photographic image of the target's face onto the head. You should also get some bits of hair, blood, or nail parings, or some article of clothing previously worn but not washed to establish the link to the target. I have found that giving the face of the doll the photographic image of the target can suffice for a link, but the more that you can acquire then the stronger the link. Once the poppet is constructed to a degree of satisfaction, then the operation may be performed.

A sigil will need to be constructed that consists of two characters or seals. The first one is constructed from the target's name, and the second is the intention of the rite. These two seals are placed on a piece of parchment and consecrated at an earlier magical working. Once charged, the sigil will sit upon the shrine until the ritual is performed.

You will also need a square piece of black tag board, approximately seven inches square, and upon this, you will paint a red triangle, either just the outline or the whole triangle shape. Place this construct into the center of the temple. This will be the focal point for the operation. Here is the ritual pattern that you can use to complete this spell. The poppet is placed on the main altar. It is best to perform this rite immediately following the new moon.

1. Consecrate the magic circle in the usual manner. This is a very solemn event, so your attitude should be sober and quiet, focused and acutely aware.
2. Perform a short meditation session to acquire the proper state of mind.
3. Perform a full votive offering to the Deities, and to the primary Deity, request assistance to achieve this rite.
4. Go to the main altar and take up the poppet and the wand, take them to the shrine, and lay the poppet before the markers of the Gods upon a metallic pentacle.
5. Consecrate the poppet with lustral water, incense, and oil.
6. Draw an invoking pentagram of spirit receptive over the poppet and project its power down into the poppet.
7. Bow over the poppet and then lean down close to its head and blow one's breath upon the head of the doll. Then say these words:

"I give you the breath of life and a consecrated existence. I give you a name, so you are called (target's name), let the Gods be aware of your charmed life imitating the life of (target's name). I give you a purpose in this life, oh (target's name), and that purpose is to (purpose of the working)."

8. Take the charged sigil and place it on the chest of the doll, saying:

"I seal this spell upon (target's name) and set the purpose of this rite, (state purpose). Thus, I hold a living model, a manikin to take upon itself the fate of (target's name)."

9. Step back from the shrine, then sit in meditation for a short period of time.
10. Stand before the poppet on the shrine, then take it to the center of the circle where the red triangle is set and lay it down with the head aligned to the apex of the triangle. Say the words:

"In the triangle, I have placed you, thereby you shall meet your fate at my hands. The triangle is the place where power and spirit converge, thus what I do to this poppet I shall do to this person. So mote it be."

11. Perform the erection of a negative vortex in the circle using the dagger. Set the four watchtowers with invoking pentagrams of spirit creative in the order of north, west, south, and east. Then draw the four watchtowers together to the center of the circle at the nadir using the dagger. Then proceed to walk around the circle in a widdershins spiral, beginning in the north and proceeding in an arc, passing the north three times, and then proceeding to the center of the circle. The raised negative energy is focused on the heart of the poppet.
12. Then sit before the poppet and build up in the mind images of what is to happen to the poppet that is now transformed into the target person. If healing and blessing is to be bestowed, then project this energy into the heart of the poppet, envisioning the parts that need to be healed, and sending love and compassion

to the doll. If evil is to be done to the target person, then perform such acts as you would like to see inflicted upon the person. You can use a rusty nail or antique knife to stab the doll repeatedly or to inflict strategic wounds in certain body parts. When performing evil upon another, it should be accompanied by hatred, anger, and as much passion as possible.

13. Once the doll has absorbed all the energy that one has to offer, then take it from the red triangle and place it upon the main altar, and cover it with a cloth of suitable color. Seal the vortex, then extinguish the lights, and leave the temple. Allow the poppet to reside on the main altar for forty-eight hours. After that time, perform a full votive offering to the Deities.

When the work is completed, divination will assist the operator to track the progress of the magical work. After a period of three weeks, then the poppet may be disposed of. If the magic was for healing and blessing, then say to the poppet:

"You are not (target's name) and I break the link that binds you to that person."

If the magic was malefic, then you may destroy the doll without breaking the link to give a greater degree of suffering to the target. Dismember the poppet and either burn or bury it.

Gathering and Dispensing Magical Energy

Magical energy resides in the body of the operator, and it is from that resource that magical powers are raised and projected to specific objectives. However, there are other sources of magical energy, and in fact, there is a universal energy that is typically triggered when an operator has achieved a certain level of raising energy from their body. Often, I have performed a magical ritual that has apparently produced far more energy than what my body alone might produce.

I believe that the reason it is necessary to ground oneself after a magical working that has produced an excess of magical energy is because there is a universal source of magical energy that ties into a magical working. This has caused me to feel more energized after a ritual than before, which requires me to siphon off that extra energy into the earth. My hypothesis is that it is the effect of resonance that triggers this universal energy and that energy is what the Eastern Sages have called *prana*, or the vital force associated with breathing.

After any powerful magical ritual performance, you will likely notice a higher level of bodily energy present than when you started the rite. If you ignore that extra energy, then it can cause a kind of intoxication. You will feel giddy, confused, and even delusional if the energy intake has been excessive.

I have seen this phenomenon quite often in my decades of magical experience, and I learned early on that it is important to learn how to ground oneself after such a ritual experience. The act of grounding is quite simple, but many either don't know that it is required or don't know how to do it. I would recommend that you perform a grounding exercise after any magical ritual work where magical energy is raised and applied to a given objective. Since working with vortices doesn't allow for the energy in the circle to be banished, using a grounding exercise becomes even more important.

Here is a simple grounding exercise.

1. Sit in meditation for a brief period.
2. Lean forward and place the palms of your hands flat upon the floor and project your bodily energy onto the earth.
3. Then eat and drink something outside of the temple.

If there is still a high energy after doing these simple steps, then go outside and put your hands into the soil or hug a tree.

There are also other types of magical energy to be found in natural settings, parks, or even wilderness areas. These places often abound in magical energy, so it becomes important to periodically visit them and to recharge yourself. Since breath is the key to energy projection and absorbing energy into the body, then finding a peaceful place to sit and meditate and purposefully breathing in the energy from that location into your body is an important method for healing and regeneration.

Absorbing energy into your body through the breath will charge you, and you can then travel back to your home and use that charge to perform a specialized magical ritual. You can also take a stone or pebble from such a location, and in a manner, take the energy associated with that place to your temple. Such tokens can be placed on the shrine to represent the energy associated with that place, and it could be called on remotely with an accompanied visualization. The possibilities for this kind of work are endless.

Seeking the Aid of Deities and Spirits

Whenever any kind of magic is to be performed, it is important to engage the Deities of your personal cult. This is particularly true concerning the primary Goddess or God with whom you are developing a personal and intimate connection. Much of the lore of Witchcraft magic seems to omit what I believe is the most important part of the work, which is to seek the aid of your Gods and engage them in your work for all magical operations that you might perform. Certainly, Christian tenets hold that asking for the help of their God through his son Jesus is quite expected and even promoted. Catholics still light votive candles and request a special mass to be said for a specific purpose, which assists in getting their God involved in their personal objectives. This kind of work should also be expected and promoted in Witchcraft, especially if that Witch is working solitary and is the sole chief of their personal religious cult.

What I have done in the rituals presented in this book is to always perform some kind of votive offering to Goddesses and Gods that are functioning as the pantheon for a solitary practice. I have done this deliberately so that it would pull the Deities into the magical work that a solitary Witch would undertake. However, there is also another approach where the full votive offering is used to request a favor or boon from one of the Deities in the pantheon. This can be done without any additional magic ritual work. You can write down the request, address it to one of your Deities, place it before the marker for that godhead on your shrine, and then proceed to work additional votive offerings and make plain your objective.

This is petitioning the Deity, and although it can be subject to the capriciousness of a God, depending on its character, it is still a potent method of gaining an objective purely through the intercession of a Deity. This is one of the benefits of having a shrine and regular liturgical practices. It makes you accessible to the Gods, but also it makes them accessible to you as well.

The only thing that is required before you seek to petition a God is to make certain that your objective is approved and accepted by the Deity. The best way to determine whether a God is in favor of what you are seeking is to use your dice or knucklebones and ask that question. If you get an affirmative, then you can proceed. If you get a negative, then further forms of divination will be required to determine what is objectionable and how to make your request acceptable.

When engaged in prayer and votive offerings you should be able to get a feeling of where your Goddess or God stands regarding a specific objective. Asking the question is the final step in this process, but engaging with your Deity through regular votive offerings will likely communicate to you the nature of your quest and how it is perceived by your Deity. As you advance in this work and over time, you might even be able to hold conversations with the Goddess or God, and then you will know their will in a direct manner, supplanting the need for dice. Until that time, using the dice to answer a question is a good idea.

When it comes to getting other spirits involved in your work, then you would have to consider performing a full evocation with its five steps, to invoke, constrain, and bind that spirit to your will and objective. That is a very complex operation, and it is beyond the scope of this work since it requires the development of a familiar spirit or the objectification of the godhead attribute of yourself. What you can do in lieu of being able to perform a full evocation is to use the power and authority of your spiritual alignment to constrain a spirit to do your will. However, I would leave that kind of work until you have all the tools available to perform an evocation.

Grand Invocation of Powers

Finally, we come to a ritual that I was given so many years ago by my first teacher and mentor, and this was before I was initiated as a Witch. I was being persecuted by the members of a local religious cult headed by a charismatic leader. Since I had told people in my high school that I was a practicing Witch, I had developed quite a notoriety, and whatever negative attention I got was my own fault. However, I was introduced to a man who claimed he was a psychic and devout Christian, and he was seeking to train divers to go and explore the Bermuda Triangle. He was the leader of a kind of New Age cult, mixing ESP and messianic Christianity into a toxic brew.

Yes, I know this sounds hard to believe, but it really happened. Anyway, I ended up dropping out of this group, and this charismatic psychic sent his teenaged minions to harass me. I needed a ritual to empower me, and I had a certain binding rite to also work, so my teacher, who sympathized with my plight, gave me a ritual to perform which would draw all four elements into the core of my being and supercharge me for any kind of follow-up working.

This was a truly powerful ritual, and I had never found its source in any book that I saw or possessed, so it became one of the most important rituals in my arsenal. I wrote it into my Book of Shadows, but it was not really any lore specific to my tradition. So, I thought that it would be a good addition to this chapter on Witchcraft magic.

What you will need to perform this ritual, although it is not required, is a black tagboard square painted with a special design. It should be large enough to stand upon, so it might be around two square feet. It is a double concentric circle with a cross dividing it into four parts. Each part has a magical word for the element and a symbol. The magical word is written between the outer circle and the inner circle, and the symbols are drawn in the inner circle. The names of the four elements are *Ignis* for the east and Fire with a symbol of the shining Sun, *Aqua* for the south and Water with a symbol of the Moon, *Caelum* for the west and Air with a six-pointed star, and *Terra* for the north and Earth with a circle crossed.

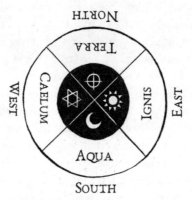

FOUR ELEMENT CIRCLE CROSS

The configuration of the elements to the watchtowers is changed for this rite for the directions east, south, and west. This represents an alternative correspondence between the four elements and the four cardinal directions. To make use of this different type of correspondence, it should be necessary to apply a set of correspondences to the four elements and the four directions. Since I had already stated that the correspondence of element to direction was an arbitrary choice and could be changed to present a different character and quality to the watchtowers, this is a prime example, and there are many more besides this one.

The key to this ritual is to visualize the four watchtowers as qualified by these four elements and to make that very clear in one's mind. Other than that, and the optional use of a tagboard platform, you should be able to perform this ritual without too much difficulty. You can use this ritual with other magical rituals to raise a great foundation of magical energy to power a critical ritual. How that is done is to perform this ritual first, then follow it with the Elemental Pentagram Energy Ritual and you will discover that the combination of these two rituals within a Lunar Mystery vortex will raise the level of magical power to a considerable extent.

Here is the ritual pattern to perform this rite.

Invoking Charge of Four Elements of Nature

1. Perform the circle consecration in the usual manner.
2. Perform a brief meditation session focusing on the objective of this work.
3. Perform the lunar full moon Mystery rite.
4. At step fourteen, proceed to the main altar and take the four elements platform to the center of the circle and align it to the four watchtowers. Draw an invoking spiral over it with the right hand.
5. Take up the dagger from the altar and proceed to the eastern watchtower and draw an invoking pentagram of Fire.
6. Proceed to the southern watchtower and draw an invoking pentagram of Water.

7. Proceed to the western watchtower and draw an invoking pentagram of Air.
8. Proceed to the northern watchtower and draw an invoking pentagram of Earth. Element pentagrams are now set to the four watchtowers.
9. Proceed to the eastern watchtower and draw a line of force from the east to the center of the circle to the platform.
10. Proceed to the southern watchtower and perform the same operation.
11. Proceed to the western watchtower and perform the same operation.
12. Proceed to the northern watchtower and perform the same operation. The crossroads are now drawn.
13. Proceed to the altar and set down the dagger and pick up the wand. Then proceed to the eastern watchtower, bow, and then face the south and proceed to slowly walk with a purposeful stride around the magic circle, proceeding deosil. Slowly arc toward the center of the circle, passing the eastern watchtower three times and then ending in the center. During this walk, use cool breathing to channel the energy, building up to a crescendo, and then projecting the energy into the nadir in the center of the circle. The solar vortex is now set.
14. Stand upon the platform, facing the east, and draw the powers of the four watchtowers into the center of one's body at the heart. Visualize these powers and breathe them into the body, feeling them accumulate there.
15. Say the following invocation.

"Sun of the East and Western Sky,
Northern lode that guards the pole.
Sea of the South my ancient blood,
Points and Elements work my goals.
All that I ask is thy desire,
All that I seek is for thy care.

*My Earth is thine, and thine my Fire,
Our Waters one, my breath thy Aire."*[23]

16. Sit upon the platform and perform the ecstatic breathing technique[24] to fully invoke the powers of the four elements.
17. Once rested and fully returned to consciousness, perform the Elemental Pentagram Energy Ritual for a specific working. Then end with a brief meditation session.
18. When all ritual work is completed, stand up, bow before the shrine, and address each Deity, thanking them for attending your Mystery ritual.

The combined ritual work is completed.

Combining rituals to achieve a greater level of magical energy is part and partial to the energy model of magic. There is still much more that could be done within the advanced working of this model, but we will end this chapter with this ritual and demonstration of what can be done using a simplified methodology incorporating the energy model of magic.

---

23 Worth, Valerie. *Crone's Book of Magical Words*. Llewellyn Publications, 2002. 120-121.

24 See Chapter Two, page 27 for Induced Ecstasy breathing technique.

CHAPTER 6

DEVELOPING AN ADVANCED MAGICAL PRACTICE

We come now to the final chapter in this book, and it is necessary for me to state that this work represents not the end of the journey, but the beginning. If you have adopted and incorporated all the rituals and practices in this book, then you have started on a path that will lead you to study and incorporate still more techniques and disciplines than what I have presented here. There are other topics to research, study, and master before you can begin the path toward a more advanced magical and liturgical practice of Witchcraft. What I have presented here is the essential foundation that will allow you the flexibility to incorporate new lore and additional disciplines to your established practice.

This book contains the basic practices for a liturgical and magical solitary practice of Witchcraft. Using the lore in this book will help you to build a private practice that will sustain and support you if your tenure in a coven or group comes to an end. It is, unfortunately, a narrow set of rituals and practices and it cannot include everything that you might find valuable and important in your journey to become more experienced and knowledgeable. That journey should be

Developing an Advanced Magical Practice

a joyous one filled with wonder and discovery. There is so much more lore and topics waiting for you to examine that I can only list a handful of the most obvious. Everyone finds their own path in the practice of Witchcraft, and although there are similarities between the directions that each person might pursue, ultimately, each person will forge a unique and independent perspective based on years of experience.

Additionally, there will be lessons to be learned—sometimes learned the hard way. You will make mistakes and use poor judgment in your life's decisions. It is said that wisdom is gained through good judgment, and that good judgment is achieved through learning the consequences of bad judgment. It is unavoidable because no one lives a perfect life. Mistakes and failures are great teaching moments, however painful and upsetting they might be. All I can do is advise you to listen to your peers and friends, the divination of the Gods, and then make your decision. Never let your emotions alone lead you to make hasty decisions. It is also said that regret is the domain of those incapable of forgetting what they have done, and what they could have done to make a wrong that occurred in the past, a right.

You will also never fail to meet adversaries and antagonists in your life. You will have to deal with ignorant and selfish fools, and sometimes, individuals who will wish to do you harm. I cannot tell you how to deal with those kinds of life struggles, but I can advocate a middle path between passivity and aggression. Be cautious when dealing with fools and miscreants, because often it is better to disengage from them and let them find their own misfortune than to be the author of their demise. However, I do not subscribe to the Wiccan Rede. I don't believe that following a rule of harming none is either practical or useful. You may need to use your magic and all other resources to deal with a spiteful antagonist who seeks to harm you, your family, friends, or loved ones. If your situation is fully justified, then you can be certain that the Gods will be on your side. Leave no stone unturned in your quest to defend yourself and your loved ones. There is no moral high ground when dealing with evil people.

Eventually, experience will teach you to be wise, and that the mistakes, conflicts, failures, and successes will help you to improve your abilities and to grow. As I said, Witches are not people of the book, they are more like people of the library. There are many resources and topics for you to explore, and it is my task in writing this book to promote other areas of study and to even promote other authors and their work for you to study. It is my hope that you will start with this book but end with having read and studied a small library by the time you get to be my age. I know that this is true for me. I own a small library, and most of the books in it I have read at least once, some of them more than once.

So, let me put together a coursework of topics and areas to research, and add to it a selection of good books for you to borrow or purchase. The idea is to expand your base of knowledge and to include other areas of practice in your practical foundation.

Here is a list of topics that it would be prudent for you to study and research.

Divination

What I have covered in this work barely touches on divination, particularly specific systems of divination. I am recommending that you master at least three of these techniques.

Tarot: You could spend the rest of your life studying the art of tarot card reading. I would recommend the book by Aleister Crowley, The Book of Thoth, which is not a book for beginners. I have recently acquired the book The Tarot: History, Symbolism, and Divination, written by Robert M. Place. He has other books published on tarot as well, so I would recommend that book if you wish to know more. Red Wheel/Weiser has a good book that teaches the classical meaning of the tarot, and it is titled The Big Book of Tarot: How to Interpret the Cards and Work with Tarot Spreads for Personal Growth, by Joan Bunning.

Astrology: You could spend a lifetime studying this discipline and still not know as much as you would like. This is a very large, multifaceted topic, but it would be a good idea to learn the basics of natal astrology. A good introduction to this discipline is a book entitled Practical Astrology for Witches and Pagans, by Ivo Dominguez Jr., and the three books written by Marion D. March and Joan McEvers, The Only Way to Learn Astrology, are still in print and available to purchase. I would also recommend Llewellyn's Moon Sign book that is published each year. This is a good resource to build up your own Moon book and to plan esbats and magical workings.

Geomancy: If you make yourself four geomancy sticks, with two indentations on one and one indentation on the other side, then you can use a very interesting and practical system of divination. The most accessible book on this subject is written by John Michael Greer and entitled The Art and Practice of Geomancy: Divination, Magic, and Earth Wisdom of the Renaissance. This is a comprehensive work and one that I recommend.

Witchcraft History and Folklore

It is a good idea to know the history of modern Witchcraft and to understand the folklore behind the Wheel of the Year. The history of the Gardnerian tradition is well-researched by Phillip Heselton. The Alexandrian tradition has been well presented in books written by the Farrars, and more recently by Jimahl Difiosa. I would also recommend the books written by Ronald Hutton, entitled *Triumph of the Moon* and *Stations of the Sun*, which are written at a university level but have served me well. The books written by Doreen Valiente are important contributions to the knowledge of Witchcraft as well. I steadfastly consider her to be the mother of the modern Witchcraft movement.

Mythology/Theology

Depending on the tradition that you are operating under or the culture of the Deities that you have chosen for your personal pantheon, there are some books that you might want to read to become acquainted with classical mythology or polytheistic theology. There is quite a range of books to be included on this topic, but I suggest a few to aid your study. To get complete exposure to classical Greek and Roman mythology, I would recommend the book *Classical Mythology: Illustrated Edition (Illustrated Classic Editions)* by Hellen A. Guerber. To gain a greater insight into Celtic mythology, I would recommend *Uncovering Celtic Mythology* by Lucas Russo, or for the Welsh ancient Deities, you can read *The Mabinogion Tetralogy: The Prince of Annwn, The Children of Llyr, The Song of Rhiannon, The Island of the Mighty* by Evangeline Walton—I had to read these stories when I was student Witch, and I enjoyed them thoroughly. Additionally, there is *The White Goddess* by Robert Graves, and *A World Full of Gods* by John Michael Greer.

Qabalah/Kabbalah

It is always a good idea to seek to know as much as possible, to add breadth to one's knowledge and expertise. The Qabalah or Kabbalah represents a Jewish mystical tradition that came to powerfully influence the practices of modern occultism and Ceremonial Magic. The spelling differences are associated with the version or variation of this topic and discipline. Kabbalah spelled with a "K" is strictly the Jewish version of this study,

Developing an Advanced Magical Practice

representing a stricter approach to Judaism and the Hebrew Bible. It is also having a revival in the Jewish community at the present time. Qabalah spelled with a "Q" is the appropriated version of this topic and discipline and represents the occultic and Christianized perspective.

Western occultists and Ceremonial Magicians mostly engage with the "Q" version of the Qabalah, allowing the Jewish version its own independent perspective and practice. While I have an opinion that the Qabalah is not particularly useful to the practice of Witchcraft, it is because the purpose and objective of the Qabalah is to produce a Talmud or an occult exegesis on sacred writings. Since Witchcraft and Paganism do not have a book of sacred writings, then such members of those traditions would not be able to engage in the full spectrum of Qabalistic studies and practices.

However, if you wish to study the Qabalah to determine if it would be useful to your own practices, then I would recommend the book *The Chicken Qabalah of Rabbi Lamed Ben Clifford*, written by Lon Milo DuQuette. You could also get a copy of a book that I wrote entitled *Magical Qabalah for Beginners*, and between these two books, you should have a good understanding of what is the Qabalah and how to use it in your studies and practices.

These four topics should open the door to gaining knowledge about other areas to research. There are so many topics and areas of research that I couldn't enumerate them all. It is also a good idea to study academic areas of archaeology, anthropology, history, psychology, astronomy, biology, physiology, neuroscience, world mythology and religion, sociology, and many other areas. You could also throw in herbology, mineralogy, and the craft skills of metallurgy, wood carving, pottery, drawing, painting, sculpture, theater, literature, poetry, and the range of artistic skills and knowledge. As you can see, the range of topics is endless, and it would be a good idea to try your hand at them all.

Duration and Qualifications for Foundational Work

I have mentioned in this book that my recommendation to you, my reader, is to perform two years of full moon Lunar Mystery rites and two years of solar sabbat rites. It is my expectation that you will also practice all the other rituals in this book, particularly the liturgical rites, with some specific magical workings over this period. You don't have to perform a binding ritual nor do poppet magic over that two-year period. The rest of the rituals are something that you should explore and experiment with over that two-year period. What I would recommend is taking the rituals from this book and writing them with whatever minor modification you might want to add to make them your own personal arsenal of rituals. This will become your own personal Book of Shadows that you will continue to develop, refine, and expand over time.

Here are some of the steps that you should take to implement the rituals and practices in this book to make them your own practices.

1. Develop your personal pantheon of Deities and assemble all the lore needed to invoke, pray to, and give homage to them. You will need to develop the images of these godheads and create or purchase markers for them. This will take a while to complete, and the two-year clock won't start to count down until you have a temple and shrine with all the tools and lore needed to properly worship these Deities.
2. Copy the ritual patterns and from them develop your own rituals. Where there are blanks associated with your personal Deities, fill them in with what you have developed. You can keep these rituals in a handwritten book or in documents on your PC. Continue to develop these rituals over time, making them more refined and efficient. It is also important to memorize these rituals

Developing an Advanced Magical Practice

as much as possible. Your expertise in performing these rituals should be such that you don't need scripts to perform them.

3. Assemble all the supplies that you will need for performing these rituals on a regular schedule. These supplies would include incense, candles, distilled water, wine or beer, bread or cakes, and anything else needed so that you can perform these rites over a period of a couple of weeks before needing to get more supplies.

4. Develop a lunar calendar and solar calendar so that you will know the times and the characteristics for these events.

5. Find a blank book, lined or unlined, to act as your magical diary. This diary should include notes about the date, time, and event or occurrence faithfully logged into it. Diary entries should also include any unique or unusual occurrences, dreams, or divination sessions. Make it a point to review this diary and put into it comments if something stands out that might have been omitted previously.

6. Once everything is ready, start your work on the first week of the month or three weeks prior to the first full moon. You should ease yourself into the disciplined practices before culminating with the first full moon working. Once you have established the start of your practices, you will be able to know when you have achieved the twenty-four months of periodic practices.

7. Make time for additional study and research periods of time. It is most important to master the art of tarot divination and to develop a facility for using dice or knucklebones. Other topics can be studied as well but allow yourself a two-hour study period (or more if possible) every week. Write down what you learned in your magical diary.

8. Explore your Pagan and Witchcraft community. Get to know the people in your local area and seek to

build a social group where you can meet and discuss magical and occult topics. Attend community-sponsored sabbat rites or local open coven events. These experiences will help you to keep your own personal practices balanced and to open yourself to adopting new techniques and methods.
9. If possible, discover ways to give assistance, material aid, and help to your community. This can include other organizations outside of the Pagan and Witchcraft communities. This gift of aid and material support can be done quietly and discreetly in the name of the Deities in your pantheon.

At the end of your two-year period of practice, you can purchase the five books in my *For Witches* series and begin to start learning and developing the practices for spirit conjuring, advanced energy work, talismanic magic, sacramental theurgy, and transformative initiation. If you have not undergone any kind of initiation, then the book *Transformative Initiation for Witches* will help to develop your own initiation ritual and then you might perform a self-initiation to seal your period of study and practice.

So, these are the steps that I would recommend that you follow for a two-year period. Once you achieve this milestone, then you will be ready to apply yourself to more advanced studies. Certainly, your abilities as a practicing Witch will be firmly established and based on experience and extensive experimentation. You won't need to believe that something is a fact; you will know it is a fact. That is the difference between someone who is just starting out and someone who is an experienced practitioner. The purpose of writing this book is to help you achieve that goal. Everything beyond it should be considered a bonus.

Developing an Advanced Magical Practice

Approaching the *For Witches* Series Study

I have written and published five books that add considerably to the practice of modern Witchcraft. All the lore presented in these books would be considered in addition to or above what is traditional and common to the practices as depicted in traditional covens or topical books. In some cases, I have given my advice and opinion on certain traditional practices that I believed should be changed or amended. It is not my place to judge the practices of other traditions or covens of Witches, but with the decades of experience that I have obtained, I feel that it is my place to give advice and opinions that will help Witchcraft to be more equitable, advanced in its practices and lore, and mature regarding its spiritual practices. I have found a way to practice and perform my Witchcraft that is a better representation of what I believe it should be, so I do practice what I preach.

Still, the material in these five books provides a system of magic and liturgical practices that is not covered by traditional practices, particularly in the study and practice of magic. I have stated quite clearly that I am not a Ceremonial Magician and that my practical magic is based on foundational practices found in an independent practice of Witchcraft. In fact, I have been singled out as someone whose magic "stinks of Witchcraft" and I can take that insult as a badge of honor. I also don't spell the word magic with a terminal "k," so I am hardly a representative of Ceremonial Magic, but still, I get that label more often than I like. I am presenting my advanced studies as based on Witchcraft, so the *For Witches* series does not stray far from the basic practices you might have acquired in a traditional coven or have particularly gained through adopting the lore in this book.

All five books are there for your study and advancement. Let me explain what is contained in each one that will add to what you have already achieved.

Spirit Conjuring for Witches: This book gives the detailed lore required to perform the evocation of spirits using a familiar spirit. That familiar spirit is your own personal godhead aligned and bound to you so that you will act through it, fully empowered like a Deity yourself.

Elemental Powers for Witches: this book takes the basic energy model of magic and extends it to include the sixteen elementals and forty qualified powers. You have used just the four elements in this book, so *Elemental Powers* teaches you the lore and practical work needed to work with more advanced energy structures enlivened by spiritual entities.

Talismanic Magic for Witches: This book teaches how to construct, charge, and empower magical talismans. Talismanic magic uses a combination of planetary and elemental magic to generate a talismanic field that is used to charge and enliven a talisman. Unlike any other kind of magical spell, a talisman sends out its intelligent guided power twenty-four hours a day, and seven days a week for perpetuity. If a Witch were to generate an array of these talismans to work magic on all the different aspects of their life that they wanted to magically charge and empower, then they would create for themself a charmed life.

Sacramental Theurgy for Witches: This book teaches how to generate and use godhead-transformed sacraments for magical purposes. It introduces the magical mass and benediction rites, amulet creation, place-markers, and thrice-consecrated

Developing an Advanced Magical Practice

tools for the Gods, and discusses in detail the methodology for impersonating and personifying a God or Goddess. It presents the methods of working magic in a sacred grove and how to plan and enact the Grand Sabbat.

Transformative Initiation for Witches: this book examines the scripted initiations found in traditional Witchcraft and presents the symbols of transformation that make them powerful rites of personal transformation. Included are the additional rituals of a third-degree ordeal, initiations for fourth- and fifth-degree, the inner order of Witchcraft, and the technique and methods for realizing and triggering transformative initiatory processes within one. The twenty-two stages of the hero and heroine's journey are matched up with the twenty-two trumps of the Major Arcana of the tarot, representing the symbols of transformation operating in all initiation rites.

These five books will teach you the art and science of a more advanced ritual magic system that you can develop and adopt into your foundational practice. What we have defined in this book will function as the required foundation needed to tackle these five books. Thus, *Mastering the Art of Witchcraft* is the first book in this series, which now contains six books instead of five.

How to approach these five books of advanced lore is completely up to you. All five of them represent a strategic addition to the lore that you already possess. I would, however, recommend that you study the books *Sacramental Theurgy for Witches* and *Transformative Initiation for Witches* together since they rely on each other for their practices and lore. It will also help you to develop your own personal initiation ritual of the four elements that could make you, if you are not yet initiated, a true initiate who is on the pathway to being a master and adept at your Craft.

After adopting the lore in these five books, there won't be much that you won't be able to accomplish spiritually, magically, and materially in your life. At that point in time, you will be the master who will teach and work with those starting out, and perhaps writing your own books that will expand the wealth of lore available to all Witches. That is my overall goal and the reason that I have spent seven years of my life writing up these books for you to read, study, enjoy, and perhaps adopt.

Competency vs. Expertise

In my many years of practicing Witchcraft, or generally living my life and working at my job, I have often bristled when someone said that I was merely competent at something. What it means to me is that I, or anyone else, have achieved a level of performance that just barely meets expectations. To say someone is competent is to indicate that they are underachievers who can do the work, but that nothing beyond that should be expected. When we apply that label to the practice of Witchcraft, it becomes a pejorative statement. In short, it is an insult!

I equate competency to complacency since it indicates that something is acceptable, expected, and even traditional. It's always the way something is done, and who am I to contradict what others say is traditional? I would expect other words of ignorance to be spoken, such as "don't rock the boat" or, "change is an unwarranted condition" or, "if it's not broken, then don't fix it." I have—especially early in my career as a Witch, or even later when encountering the faux orthodoxy—discovered that my ideas go against the grain of traditional practices. I have been called an anti-traditionalist or even an apostate for talking about what I felt needed to be changed in the practice of Witchcraft. I have experienced resistance and push-back from traditional practitioners, and it has even served me losses in my professional career.

Developing an Advanced Magical Practice

It would appear that I am promoting ideas and practices that are blasphemous and irreligious, even though my elder peers in the various traditions are some of my biggest supporters. This is a quandary and even a conundrum for me to puzzle over when I am not busy writing, living, loving, and practicing magic, which isn't often. What seems to be happening to me and others is the distinction between competency and expertise. I am promoting that my fellow members of the Witchcraft movement discard any hint of competency and follow the path to build their own basis of expertise. I would rather engage with experts than have to deal with complacent and competent practitioners.

When there are new directions to explore, new ritual lore to develop and experiment with, and whole areas to research and understand, then why would anyone be happy to remain the same? Where is the challenge with orthodoxy? Maintenance is, in my opinion, a lazy way to resist any kind of change, even ones that would open whole new worlds to explore and experience. Complacency is a state of stasis, and it breeds stagnation, corruption, and ultimately, collapse. I am not interested in seeing Witchcraft go in that direction, so I am pushing for change, expansion, new development, and the addition of new lore. I believe that the tradition of Witchcraft is too young, incomplete, and too shallow yet to succumb to orthodoxy. So, there is no reason to keep the tradition as it was given to us and to simply maintain it thereafter.

What I have done in publishing these books is to promote my vision of a Witchcraft that is continually changing and developing itself. Perhaps over the next few hundred years, our religion might mature enough to adopt an orthodoxy, but I seriously doubt it. I am promoting change, even for the sake of change, so that there will always be doors to be opened and new perspectives to be discovered. It is my goal to stimulate individuals and groups so that we can create a large body of experts. When that goal is met, there won't be anything that we cannot accomplish in the present time, and in the future, too.

WITCHCRAFT PATH: LIVING RELIGION AND MAGIC

The core practice in this book consists of the regular liturgies involving and engaging with the personal cult of the Deities of Witchcraft. These Goddesses and Gods function as the soul and axis of an individual religious and magical praxis. They are the living spiritual heart of what a Witch does on a regular basis. Any magic, material and spiritual rewards, a life lived in plenty, and good health come from these Gods. It is expected then that all our love, passion, and zest for life flows into our service to the Deities. This relationship is very much unlike any other religion that I have ever studied or heard about. So many religions are material and emotional siphons that often seem to give little in return. Perhaps these faiths may bolster beliefs plagued by insecurities, inequality, and most of all, the inevitable experience of death itself. Yet Witchcraft, especially when practiced by a solitary Witch seems to give back even more than it takes from the practitioner.

If the Gods live in our shrine and enliven our magical and liturgical work, then we can live our lives close to their immanent emanations that reward us with material-based grace. We seek to fulfill our obligations to our Gods, but we don't always successfully achieve the uniform and continuous engagement that we should. Our Gods don't rebuke or punish us for our failings since they seek to encourage our engagement with them to generate the kind of magical existence that we deem important and necessary. We are mortal and subject, as all living things, to dissolution and death. We are frail creatures who are flawed and imperfect, but still a singular attribute of nature. That fact alone gives the Goddesses and Gods of Witchcraft the means to champion us, to uplift us when we are down, and to share briefly in our mortality as we share briefly in their godhood.

If the Gods are the core of our work, then what of magic? In other religions, magic is either outlawed or considered the provenance of the Deity and not to be copied or emulated by the members. Specialized individuals are given some special privileges, but the magic is kept for the Deity's creative use and despotic control of living beings alone. However, in Witchcraft, the magic of the Gods is shared with its members, enshrouding them with the noumena of psychic transformation and material transmutation. We are their agents in the world, and our magical and liturgical work is where they make their will manifest in the greater world of the collective. This relationship is based on the common thread that unites us all—nature. This is because our Deities are not apart and separate from nature; they are immersed in nature.

Witchcraft magic is then the play of the numinous powers of the Gods transforming the psychic and material world, acting through us, their agents. We deploy the magic, and through us, the Gods change the world in psychic and material ways. We are the conduit of the Gods acting from their domain in the world of Spirit through us into the material world. All is nature, and the soul of nature is the collective of the Gods acting as a singularity throughout the domain of consciousness and material existence. Therefore, we Witches are the life and power of the Gods acting in the material world. There are no divisions in that collective, for all is one and united. Some have called this the Great Spirit, or have characterized it as the monotheistic God, but in truth, it is the great Mystery that cannot be realized, named, or understood by individual minds.

Our path as members of a living relationship between our Gods and our mortal lives, through the agency of magic and psychic transformation, is to function as the divine mediators of this very special religion, so unlike any other. As we develop ourselves, we also develop our Gods; as we are successful in our lives, so, too, the Gods are successful. We come into our life path as unwitting agents, witnesses, and mediators for this host of Deities; but we leave this world as members of that divine host, having transformed our spiritual nature to be like the Gods.

We are absorbed back into that divine host and achieve our objective, to become one with all things within our world. Death brings enlightenment and releases our mortal coil with this world, but all that we were and are becomes an eternal living one-ness, where all distinctions are dissolved, and all attributes absorbed into it. We are born from nature and to it we return, and that soul of nature is the unity of all beings, even the Gods. Such is the life and death of a Witch in the Craft of the Wise.

Frater Barrabbas

APPENDIX

PANTHEON DEVELOPMENT

I FELT THAT PRODUCING an example of building a Witchcraft pantheon of Deities would be necessary to show how to approach this task. I also believed that presenting two examples of the kind of descriptions—hymns and prayers—short and long invocations needed to develop a liturgical practice would also be necessary.

These tasks are probably going to be the most difficult to do, so I felt an obligation to give some examples to help show the way. Keep in mind that the work of developing a pantheon will not be something that you will be able to accomplish in a short time. You might be able to establish the basics and get a good start on this work, but over time, you will revise, amend, and refine it. This is an evolving process that will take a while to complete. You will need to have the basics down before you can start the work of an independent and solitary Witch, and there is no hurry to get this done. It should be the kind of work that brings you joy, wonder, and warm satisfaction when completed.

Approaching the pantheon of Witchcraft pulls together Deities that seem separate and distinct, but you are making them into a family of related Goddesses and Gods who interact with each other. This is easier done when dealing with a known collection of Deities from a specific culture, be that Welsh, Irish, Celtic, Germanic, Norse, Roman, Greek, Ugaritic, Mesopotamian, or Egyptian. However, in my example, I wanted to approach the known Deities of Witchcraft and build a pantheon out of that group. While most of the Gardnerian-influenced coven traditions had a kind of confusing duo-theological structure of primary Goddess and God with many attributes, this settled on Diana, Lucifer-Helios, and Cernunnos-Herne, a horned God. While the *Vangello* or *Gospel of Aradia* mentions Diana and Lucifer, the Gardnerians added or exchanged the sun God for a horned God in their theological structure. This could be confusing, but most pantheons are somewhat confusing with various conflicting myths, relationships, and stories.

What I decided to do is build a pantheon as an example from the Gardnerian Witchcraft creed and develop it into a workable theological structure. Since some folks will not be interested in the task of investing in foreign cultures, myths, and languages, I decided to work with the common collection of Witchcraft Deities and use the English language as my means of writing hymns, prayers, and invocations. Allow me to demonstrate how this might be done using just the Goddesses and Gods of Witchcraft. My approach is highly creative, so there might be very little from a theological or historical precedence to base my pantheon. Here is the pantheon as I envision it.

The primary Deities are Diana, Moon Goddess; Lucifer, the Sun God; and Herne, the Horned God. Diana and Lucifer are brother and sister, and they are celestial Deities. Herne, the Horned God, Lord of the Trees, and Keeper of the Underworld, is a God that seasonally dies and is reborn. He is a lintel godhead, representing both life and death. Diana, who is also the huntress, is the mother of all beasts and the protector of childbirth and mothers. Diana and Herne are lovers, but there is also an incestuous relationship between Diana and Lucifer. Diana has a daughter named Aradia, but her designated father is unclear, being either Lucifer or

Herne. She is the messenger and teacher of the Witches and is both mortal and immortal. Diana also has a son-like mortal lover named Adonis (Acteon), who she accidentally kills and resurrects. So, in my imagination, this is the primary family of the Witchcraft Deities and their relationships.

Since Diana is the Goddess of the Moon, she is seen as being multiforme, because the Moon is always changing its phases. We can see these phases in four parts or three parts if we see them as faces. The new moon is represented by a veil or the face of darkness, so we could say that Diana as the Moon Goddess is a three-part or faced Deity. Of course, making her three-part would also be connecting her to Hecate, the underworld Goddess, and Queen of the Witches. Hecate could then be seen as an aspect of Diana in her dark face phase, and because Witches have been associated with Hecate in antiquity. In our modern pantheon, we could make that a feature of the Moon Goddess. That would bring in a lot of other lore into the guise of Diana, and some purists would object to my logic, but this is a private pantheon of my own making, so these kinds of connections are allowed.

Other Deities would be Gaia, the life force of the planet, and her son, the Green Man, who is the personification of the world of flora and vegetation. I have personally met the Green Man in some of my sacred grove experiences, so I know for a fact that he exists and is part of this pantheon. I would suspect that since his green nature is due to chlorophyll, his father would be the Sun God, mating with Gaia. Then there are the demigods of the Oak King and the Holly King, who represent the vegetative blessings of the seasonal year. They are supposed to be engaged in eternal conflict, so I would suppose that they are fraternal twins. There are the four Dread Lords, who are unnamed, but I have taken the liberty of identifying them with the four Demon Kings or Chiefs, and there are the four Wind (Weather) Gods who ward the cardinal directions along with the Demon Kings. Each convenstead locality would also have its own local Deities, representing the various features of the land upon which it resides. A great tree, hills, lakes, swamps, rivers, springs, underground aquifers, creeks, and various other topological qualities would be perceived as Deities.

A final addition to this pantheon represents the merging, blending, and union of all the various Deities into a singular and unnamed entity that is perceived as the source of everything and the prominent Mystery that pervades the world in which we live. The Gardnerians called this state of union the Dreighton of ancient provenance, but have otherwise left it without any further definition.

So, what we have are the Deities Diana, Lucifer, Herne, Aradia, and Adonis as the basic family of Goddesses and Gods. These five godheads would represent the primary collection of Deities, and Diana and Herne would be the primary pair. As a male perceived gendered Witch (or Warlock, if you prefer) whose inclination is heterosexual, I would take on the role of Herne and seek to be intimate with Diana. My focus would be worshipping Diana as her lover, and I would assume the guise of Herne, the horned God. I might go so far as to wear an antlered headdress or mask and other garb and seek to be one with him to approach her as a proper suitor.

Now that I have established the groundwork identifying the pantheon of Deities in my Witchcraft theological collective and my role toward my chosen primary Goddess and God, I would need to develop this pantheon so it would become a workable liturgical system. I would need to develop detailed descriptions of the primary and ancillary Deities, then write a short hymn to them, followed by a short invocation to summon their presence for a votive rite and offering. I would also need to write up a more extensive communion invocation for the Goddess Diana and the God Herne. With all these different texts developed, I would place them into a single folder that would become the core of my personal Book of Shadows.

However, for our example here, I will show these four steps for just Diana and Herne. Since there is a lot of mythology about the Roman Goddess Diana and the Greek Goddess

Artemis, I would need to do some research to develop my ideas about them to create a modern synthesis that I would use. Herne, also known obscurely as Cernunnos, has very few cultural or antique sources, so here I would either defer to what the community has defined as Herne the Horned God, or I would have to use my creative imagination.

At the end of this process, much of what would be collected and written would be more creative imagination than actual historical precedence. What I would be producing is for my own use, and it would not need to be judged by my peers unless I felt obliged to reveal it to them. The Gods themselves would likely communicate ideas about themselves that would be added to this lore. So, this lore that I would develop could be personal and subject to unverified personal gnosis, which, for a personal approach to Deity, is completely acceptable.

Let us start with Diana. Here are her various epithets and titles. As you can see, we are merging Diana, Artemis, and Hecate into a single Goddess.

Diana the Goddess of the Moon, Protector of Motherhood and Birth, Queen of Witches, Traveler with Many Faces, Sister of the Sun, Divine Huntress, Virginal, Threefold, Seer and Teacher of Hidden things, Queen of Magic and Rebirth, Mother of All Living Creatures, Many Breasted.

DESCRIPTION AND SUITABLE OFFERINGS: A beautiful young maid armed with bow and arrows, dressed as a male in hunting clothes, virginal and immortal. She has very fair white skin, long black tresses always braided and bound, green eyes, and a serious expression and attitude. She also appears as a pregnant mother with full breasts and belly; and as an old hag with long white hair, skeletally thin, and body bent with age, a wrinkled face with an overlong nose, with pendulous breasts. Her guise depends on the phase of the Moon. Her offerings are lunar in nature, such as milk or cream, cheese, white mushrooms, or unleavened bread. She can be offered wine if it is blood red and tart, and cake if it is pale or yellow. Offerings of meat (venison, beef, lamb, goat, or pork) are accepted only if they are uncooked and bloody. Her incense offerings are dragon's blood or myrrh. Her floral offerings are the lily and the rose entwined.

HYMN: *I sing to you, O Diana, Goddess of Witches who are your hidden children, the praises of my people rise to you on high. When the Moon is full, you delight us with your mysterious light and offer us your protection in childbirth, the blessings of the wild hunt, and the abundance of domestic animals. We adore you because you give us these blessings and illuminations and teach us the mysteries of magic.*

SHORT INVOCATION: *O Diana, Queen of Witches, I summon you with praise, love, and offerings, to come down from the sky and partake of these offerings made in your name. Come forth, oh beauteous one, ever virgin and always divine mother, and grace us with your presence.*

Pantheon Development

Long Invocation: *O Great Goddess of the Moon, Queen of Witches, mother of my magical inspiration. I yearn for your embrace and to be enraptured in your arms. I am like the great Horned One who welcomed you into his underworld above. I am like your mortal lover, resurrected when he faced death. Come to me, oh Mighty One, ever-virgin and all-mother, and bless these offerings with your essence, so we might become one with you in body and spirit.*

As you can see, the hymns and invocations should be short and easy to memorize. The long invocation will require some passion and emotional angst to entice the Goddess to make an appearance and bless the sacraments.

Then we will proceed to Herne the Horned God, and here we will need a lot more imagination. However, the pattern established for Diana would be repeated for Herne as well. Also, keep in mind that as the priest, I would be approaching Herne to emulate him so that I might approach the Goddess as her lover. Although it is not emphasized in the votive rite or the full moon Mystery, I would assume the guise of Herne prior to invoking the Goddess Diana to bless the sacraments, so there is a difference in roles used in these texts.

> *Herne the Horned God, Lord of the Trees, Master of the Wild Hunt, Lord of Misrule, Lord of the Underworld and Guide of the Dead, God of Death and Rebirth, Master of the Magic of the Powers of Darkness and Light, Teacher and Deceiver, Wearer of Masks, Lord of the Carnivale, Beloved of the Moon Goddess.*

DESCRIPTION AND SUITABLE OFFERINGS: A virile, muscular, and hairy naked man with the markings of a roebuck and a fully erect penis. He is wearing a mask and horn crown, standing in the forest mist between the world of the living and the dead. He is a dying God that shares mortality with humankind but also has the power of rebirth. He is the Lord of the Trees and Lord of the Underworld, symbolizing the doorway between the worlds of light and darkness, life and death. He is also a hunter and the hunted, the champion, and the victim; he gives his life so that others might live and herds the dead, preparing them for rebirth. Herne is also the Master of the Hunt and the Lord of Misrule, representing the chaos associated with the opening of the lintel doorway between worlds. He teaches through suffering and pain, but also pleasure, and he can be deceptive, tricky, and deceitful. His offerings are ale or stout, black pumpernickel or dark rye bread, brown mushrooms, lentils, olives, and pomegranates. His incense is musk, patchouli, or frankincense. His flowers are antler sheds, fly agaric mushrooms, and moss.

HYMN: *I sing to you, O Herne, Horned God, and Lord of the Trees, and I bow before your erect phallus and feral colorings. I make the sign of the horn and seek to receive your mark in turn. O*

Pantheon Development

beauteous fawn of my dreams, my heart is open to you. Teach me the ways of the powers of light and darkness, show me the secrets of rebirth. Open the keyless door to your mysteries that I might enter and become your acolyte.

SHORT INVOCATION: *O Herne, Horned God and Lord of the Trees, I summon you with praise, lust, and offerings, to come forth from your hidden domain and partake of these offerings made in your name. Come forth, oh virile one, Dying God, hunter and hunted, and grace us with your presence.*

LONG INVOCATION: *O Great Horned God, Herne, Lord of the Trees and Master of the Underworld. I call you down to me and I assume the position before you to be taken and be made one. I passionately adore you and seek to fully know you! Let me assume your guise and feel the power of your desire, as I approach the Goddess of the Moon. I give you your sign and I receive your mark. May it be so!*

The long invocation is used so that I might become one with Herne and characterize my approach to the Goddess Diana as her consort and lover. Since there is a bisexual quality to Herne, the invitation could be received in a very intimate fashion, and as his representative, I should be able to deal with that in whatever manner it manifests.

I have given some good examples of how to develop a pantheon and how to write up the texts that are needed to help you properly worship these Deities. It is my hope that armed with these examples, you might be able to develop your own texts and devotional practice, which I believe is central to any kind of independent practice of Witchcraft.

BIBLIOGRAPHY

Betz, Hans Dieter. *The Greek Magical Papyri in Translation.* University of Chicago Press, 1986.

Bunning, Joan. *The Big Book of Tarot: How to Interpret the Cards and Work with Tarot Spreads for Personal Growth.* Red Wheel Weiser, 2019.

Crowley, Aleister. *The Book of Thoth.* Weiser Books, 1944.

Del Rabina, Antonio Venitiana. Translated by Gretchen Rudy. *The Grand Grimoire.* Trident Books, 1996.

Dominguez, Ivo, Jr. *Practical Astrology for Witches and Pagans.* Red Wheel Weiser, 2016.

DuQuette, Lon Milo. *The Chicken Qabalah of Rabbi Lamed Ben Clifford.* Red Wheel Weiser, 2010.

Farrar, Stewart and Janet. *A Witches' Bible: The Complete Witches' Handbook.* Phoenix Publishing, 1996.

Frater Barrabbas. *Transformative Initiation for Witches.* Crossed Crow Books, 2024.

—. *Elemental Power for Witches.* Llewellyn Publications, 2021.

—. *Spirit Conjuring for Witches.* Llewellyn Publications, 2017.

—. *Magical Qabalah for Beginners.* Llewellyn Publications, 2013.

Guerber, Helen A. *Classical Mythology: Illustrated Edition.* Sterling Publishing Company, Inc., 2018.

Graves, Robert. *The White Goddess: A Historical Grammar of Poetic Myth.* Farrar, Straus, and Giroux, 1972.

Greer, John Michael. *A World Full of Gods.* ADF Publications, 2005.

—. *The Art and Practice of Geomancy.* Red Wheel Weiser, 2009.

Huson, Paul. *Mastering Witchcraft: A Practical Guide for Witches, Warlocks and Covens.* G. P. Putman and Sons, 1970.

Hutton, Ronald. *The Triumph of the Moon.* OUP Oxford, 2019.

March, Marion D., and Joan McEvers. *The Only Way to Learn Astrology*. ACS Publications, 2008.

Place, Robert Michael. *The Tarot: History, Symbolism, and Divination*. Penguin, 2005.

Russo, Lucas. *Uncovering Celic Mythology*. JCG Publishing, 2021.

Trithemius, Johannes. *Polygraphia*. c.1499.

Walton, Evangeline. *The Mabinogion Tetralogy: The Prince of Annwn (1974), The Children of Llyr (1971), The Song of Rhiannon (1972), The Island of the Mighty (1964)*. The Overlook Press/Peter Mayer Publishers, Inc., 2012

Worth, Valerie. *Crone's Book of Magical Words*. Llewellyn Publications, 2002.

INDEX

A

Air, 14, 16–17, 26, 30, 32, 36, 38, 40–41, 43, 55, 78–79, 83, 116, 118
Athame, 16–17, 30, 77

B

Banish, 13, 17, 30, 40, 55, 79–80, 82, 87, 112
Bellows Breath, 26–27, 88
Bind, 95, 97–103, 111, 115, 126
Blessing, 30, 36–37, 43, 45, 49, 51, 53, 60–62, 69, 76–77, 104, 107, 110–111, 139, 142–144
Breath, 24–27, 30, 88, 107, 109, 113, 119

C

Cardinal Directions, 12–13, 16, 33–34, 36, 117, 139
Cauldron, 16, 18, 31, 104
Chalice, 16, 18–19, 31, 33, 37–38, 61–62
Charging, 19, 27, 30–31, 34, 36–37, 55, 58, 61, 76–77, 80, 85, 88, 109–110, 113, 117, 130
Circle, 12–15, 30–37, 39–40, 47, 53, 55–59, 65, 67, 76, 79–80, 82–83, 85–92, 102, 109–110, 112, 116–118
Communion, 9, 18–19, 51, 55, 57, 59–61, 63, 76, 85, 140
Concentration, 24, 28
Cone of Power, 55, 86, 90
Consecration, 15, 17–20, 30–37, 47, 53, 56, 58, 65, 67, 76–77, 80, 86–87, 90–91, 102, 109, 117, 130
Constraining, 98–99, 115
Contemplation, 10, 24, 29, 51
Cool Breathing, 26–27, 35, 38, 57, 59, 78, 88, 118
Crystal, 16, 19, 47, 65, 67

D

Dagger, 16–17, 26, 30–31, 33–34, 36–39, 56, 58–59, 76–78, 87–88, 103, 110, 117–118

Demon Chiefs, 14–15
Demons, 10, 14–15, 139
Deosil, 34–36, 38, 55, 57–59, 78, 82, 87–88, 118
Dice, 47, 90, 114–115, 127
Direction, 4, 12–16, 19, 33–36, 40, 55, 63, 82, 91, 116–117, 121, 133, 139
Divination, 3, 18, 24, 35, 41, 46–48, 72–73, 90–93, 104, 111, 114, 121–123, 127

E

Earth, 8, 11, 14, 16, 31–32, 36, 39, 41–43, 79–80, 83, 112, 116, 118–119, 123
Elemental Pentagram, 86–87, 99, 117, 119
Elementals, 14–16, 30, 34, 41, 54, 57, 79, 82–84, 86–87, 89, 96, 99, 117, 119, 130
Energy, 12, 19, 24, 26–28, 30–31, 34–35, 38–41, 54–60, 73–74, 76, 78–80, 82–90, 96, 98–99, 102, 110–113, 117–119, 128, 130
Esbat, 40–42, 44, 53–54, 56–57, 123
Ethics, 73

F

Fire, 12, 14, 16, 30, 32, 39, 41, 43, 54–56, 79–80, 83, 116–117, 119

For Witches, 47, 54, 66, 84, 123, 128–131
Full Moon, 40–41, 44, 51, 53–54, 56–57, 74, 76–77, 85–87, 91, 117, 126–127, 144

G

Geomancy, 47, 123
Grand Bewitchment, 107–108
Grand Invocation, 115

H

Henotheism, 63
Hymn, 9, 23, 45, 49–53, 106, 137–138, 140, 142–144

I

Incantation, 104, 106
Induced Ecstasy, 27, 119
Invocation, 9, 23, 45, 49, 51, 53, 60–63, 92, 104, 115, 118, 137–138, 140, 142–143, 145
Invoking Charge, 117

K

Knucklebones, 90, 114, 127

L

License to Depart, 30, 40, 92, 100
Lunar Calendar, 127

INDEX

M

Meditation, 9, 21, 23–25, 27–29, 35, 37, 50–54, 56, 58, 61, 63, 71, 91, 109–110, 112–113, 117, 119

N

New Moon, 40–41, 44, 74, 109, 139

O

Offering, 9, 15, 18–19, 21, 33, 35, 45, 49, 51–53, 55, 57–60, 62–65, 67–68, 91, 102, 109, 111, 114, 140, 142–145

P

Pagan, 6–8, 11, 20, 41, 49, 63, 123, 127–128
Pagan Culture, 11
Pantheon, 2, 6, 33, 37, 45, 49–50, 52–53, 60, 63, 65–67, 90–91, 99, 114, 124, 126, 128, 137–141, 143, 145, 147
Pentacle, 16, 19, 31, 37–38, 77, 109
Pentagram, 14–15, 19, 26, 31, 33–34, 36, 38–40, 55–56, 58, 62, 73, 76, 78–80, 82–84, 86–87, 90, 99, 109–110, 117–119

Polytheism, 6
Poppet, 94–95, 107–111, 126
Power, 9, 14–19, 24, 30–31, 35–36, 38, 49, 54–55, 60–61, 65, 67, 69, 71, 77–79, 83–84, 86–90, 94–95, 97–100, 103–106, 109–111, 115, 117–119, 130, 135, 144–145
Practical Rules, 71, 89
Prayer, 9, 49–54, 58, 63, 91–92, 114, 137–138

R

Releasing, 35, 84, 97–98, 100, 103, 136
Rule of Contagion, 95
Rule of Similarity, 95, 107
Rune, 47, 92

S

Sabbat, 40, 42–44, 51, 53–54, 57–59, 126, 128, 131
Sacral Nudity, 20–21
Sacred Space, 12, 20, 23, 30, 32–36, 49–53, 55, 57, 59, 61, 63, 65, 67, 90–91
Self-Dedication, 66
Shrine, 12, 15, 20, 32–33, 37, 40, 45, 52–54, 57, 59–65, 67, 92, 101–102, 109–110, 113–114, 119, 126, 134
Sigil, 18, 73, 83–89, 95, 109–110
Solar Calendar, 23, 40, 127

Spell, 1, 35, 72, 86, 94, 97, 104, 107–110, 129–130

Spiral, 17, 26, 30–31, 34–35, 55, 57–59, 77–80, 82–83, 87, 110, 117

Widdershins, 34–35, 55, 57–59, 82, 88, 110

Witchcraft Path, 134

T

Tarot, 47, 122–123, 127, 131

Temple, 3, 10–15, 17, 19–20, 22–23, 25, 32–39, 49, 53, 55–56, 58, 65, 103, 105, 109, 111–113, 126

Thanksgiving, 43, 59, 100

Tool Consecration, 76

Trance, 23–24, 26–27, 63, 71

V

Visualization, 24, 28, 31, 38, 79, 87, 113, 117–118

Vortex, 54–59, 90, 110–112, 117–118

Votive Offering, 9, 33, 35, 51–53, 55, 58, 63, 67, 91, 102, 109, 111, 114

W

Watchtower, 12–14, 32–34, 36–40, 55–59, 64, 87–89, 101–102, 110, 116–118

Water, 14, 16, 18–20, 30–32, 36–37, 39, 41, 43, 47, 76–77, 79, 83, 109, 116–117, 119, 127